BadAsstronauts

ALSO BY GRADY HENDRIX

FICTION

The Final Girl Support Group

The Southern Book Club's Guide to Slaying Vampires

We Sold Our Souls

My Best Friend's Exorcism

Horrorstör

SHORT FICTION

*BadAsstronauts**

*Dead Leprechauns & Devil Cats: Strange Tales of the White Street Society**

NON-FICTION

These Fists Break Bricks: How Kung Fu Movies Swept America and Changed the World (with Chris Poggiali)

Paperbacks from Hell: The Twisted History of '70s and '80s Horror Fiction (with Will Errickson)

*available as a JABberwocky ebook

BadAsstronauts

Grady Hendrix

JABberwocky Literary Agency, Inc.

BadAsstronauts

Published in 2022 by JABberwocky Literary Agency, Inc.
Originally published in 2012 as *Occupy Space*.

Cover art by Doogie Horner.

Paperback ISBN 978-1-625675-58-3
Ebook ISBN 978-1-625675-57-6

INTRODUCTION

I self-published the book you're reading back in 2011 under the title *Occupy Space*. A decade later I re-read it, and even though I thought it still held up, it needed a polish. In part that's because I was a different person when I wrote it, and in part it's because the world was a different place. In 2011, the American economy still seemed broken in the wake of the 2008 global financial crisis. No one had work, unemployment had been hovering around ten percent for years, and it felt like what had gotten broken wasn't going to get fixed anytime soon. Overdoses from heroin and oxycontin were spiking across rural America, the Tohoku Earthquake in Japan caused the Fukushima Daiichi nuclear power plant to go into meltdown, leading to the evacuation of over one hundred fifty thousand people, and Representative Gabby Giffords (D-Arizona) and nineteen other people were shot at a public event. Six of them died, including a federal judge and a nine-year-old girl.

I felt frustration and stagnation in my personal life, too. Before 2008, I'd made a great living writing cultural coverage as a freelance journalist. I reviewed books and movies for a couple of places, wrote the occasional magazine article, covered the Asian film business for *Variety* on a blog called Kaiju Shakedown that was, for a while, their most popular online feature. I wrote photo captions and TV schedule descriptions, film festival catalogue copy, and humor pieces. I did anything that brought in a check. But the 2008 financial crisis caused newsrooms to cut back their budgets and my kind of freelance work became a thing of the past. 2009 saw New York City transformed into a scene from the zombie apocalypse with starving freelancers wandering the streets offering to write articles for free, as long as it featured their byline.

Too many writers jammed too few editors' inboxes with pleas for work, but there wasn't any. Writers were dying like dogs and I only had one skill: writing. Not knowing what else to do, I decided to double down and try fiction. I got into the Clarion Science Fiction and Fantasy Writers' Workshop out in San Diego, and those six weeks would change my life, but not for a while. I came back to New York City and went back to scraping together a living from whatever freelance work I could scrounge up. I wrote press releases for horror movies. I landed a couple of interviews at *GQ*. I wrote a ton of articles for Tor.com, which paid $25 each — writing four of those in a month covered my groceries.

However, fiction writing slowly started to happen.

My best friend from high school landed a contract for a YA trilogy and then she got pregnant. When her deadline started breathing down her neck, she asked if I wanted to co-author them and I jumped at the chance. We had a blast writing the first two books, but her editor hated the fact that she'd brought me on board and hated what we were writing. She insisted that we downsize one female character's dreams from becoming an architect to becoming a fashion designer. She vetoed scenes because the main characters' clothes got too dirty. She insisted that our books, set in the South and focusing on the tensions between a Black and white family, not use the word "white" to identify characters.

Around the same time, my wife, who's a chef, sold a cookbook to a big publisher. She hadn't wanted to write a cookbook because there are too many of them out there already, and most of them are fully disposable with their industry standard food pinup photos and their cookie cutter stories about learning to cook at grandma's knee. But her restaurant was doing great and publishers kept asking her to write one, and it was getting harder and harder to say no to the money. We were talking about it one night, and one of us said, "The only reason to do a cookbook would be to do something totally stupid, like a comic book cookbook." Which turned out to be the right idea. Somehow, we convinced Ryan Dulavey (*Action Philosophers*) to illustrate it and we sold it to a publisher. The only problem?

At our first editorial meeting the editor said, "So... what if this wasn't a graphic novel?" She'd bought it, apparently, to keep anyone else from buying it. She had zero interest in doing a graphic novel cookbook and every step of the process became a battle. I had two books in progress but both of them involved group decisions, extreme diplomacy, and endless notes that resulted in rewrite after rewrite. I wanted to write something just for myself where I could blow off steam.

At the time, self-publishing was hot. The internet swarmed with stories of people making thousands, if not tens of thousands, if not hundreds of thousands, of dollars every month with their self-published sci-fi and crime ebooks. I carefully analyzed the market and spent a long time coming up with what turned out to be a terrible strategy to self-publish my first book, *Satan Loves You*. All my hard work resulted in a book absolutely no one wanted to read. Each month I made about $20 from it, no matter how many giveaways I did, or what kind of pricing model I tried, or how many free copies I used to seed sales.

I felt trapped, out of options, and out of hope.

In the summer of 2011, NASA flew its final Space Shuttle mission, then mothballed the program and it felt symbolic. I wasn't a big tech guy, but the Space Shuttle was a part of my life. The first Shuttle mission launched in 1981 when I was nine years old, and I remember poring over the diagrams and drawings of the Shuttle that were published in every magazine and newspaper. I remember when the *Challenger* blew up and when Skylab came down, I remember when the International Space Station got put together. And now, the entire program was gone. America had closed the door on space, and the planet suddenly felt a whole lot smaller.

When one of my big sisters had left for college years before, she'd left behind a few of Robert Heinlein's "juveniles," and I inherited them because no one else cared. I could barely claw my way to a C in any science class no matter how hard I worked, but these books hooked me with their odes to the joys of engineering, extremely long chapters about plotting trajectories and orbits, and their emphasis on self-reliance and astrophysics. I read them over and over again, especially *Space Cadet* and *Have Space Suit–Will Travel*, and for some reason they made a better future seem possible, as long as we had the right set of hex wrenches. I was never a huge science fiction fan, but in September 2011, Neal Stephenson wrote an essay for *World Policy Journal*, claiming we'd given up on big ideas and turned our backs on the future. It felt like a eulogy spoken at a particularly poorly attended funeral, but it said a lot of what I was feeling. My career wasn't going anywhere, and the world felt like a big bowl of fail. Hope seemed like something for suckers. It felt like at any moment someone was going to come along and turn out the lights.

Then came Occupy Wall Street. The Arab Spring had started percolating at the end of 2010 and spread across the Middle East in 2011. Stories of crowds standing up to their governments armed with nothing more than complete fearlessness, strength in numbers, and their smartphones were the first good thing I remember happening back then. Of course, it was happening in Egypt and Tunisia and had nothing to do with my everyday life, but then, on September 17, 2011, protesters occupied Zuccotti Park near Wall Street and the police couldn't seem to shake them. Matching protests broke out across the country, frustrating old people with their lack of leadership and demands for nothing less than total systemic change, and inspiring people like me who'd felt their backs against the wall. Suddenly, people were talking about income inequality and the minimum wage, about corporate control of politics, and the financial services sector becoming the tail that wagged the American dog.

Frustrated cops pepper sprayed peaceful protesters in the face, stormed their encampments in riot gear, and bulldozed their free libraries. I made a couple of supply runs from my wife's restaurant to Zuccotti Park and the energy was electrifying. It felt like the future, and it shot lightning through my veins. For the first time in a long while, I felt hope. I wanted to make my own contribution to the cause but, while I'd done a lot of protesting back in the day, I was trying to be a writer now, so it made sense that what I'd do would be to write.

I wanted to write a book where people stepped up and took back their future, a book where people who'd been crushed by the economy used engineering and the good old American superpowers of Building Shit and Banging Things with Wrenches to weave a magic spell that changed the world. I was allergic to stories about Chosen Ones fixing everything with a magic wand. I'd grown up in a world of backyard mechanics and garage tinkerers, and I wondered what would happen if they came together in a loosely affiliated network to take us all back into space. If we dedicated ourselves to being better than ourselves rather than worse. I wanted to see the energy of the Occupy movement move from political protest and the metaphorical building of the future into the actual, real life, physical building of a better tomorrow.

I wrote *Occupy Space* in a single burst of energy over the course of three months, and I self-published it with a great cover featuring the image of a solidarity fist and rocket ship designed by my friend (and frequent screenplay co-author) Nick Rucka and... no one cared. It did about the same business as *Satan Loves You*. My career continued to limp along, the young adult books got no support from the publisher and did so little business they never hired us to write the third. The *Dirt Candy* cookbook got a knife in the ribs when it received less than zero marketing support from its publisher. The Arab Spring gave way to what's known as the Arab Winter, as many of its gains were rolled back. And on November 15, 2011, cops waded into the Zuccotti Park encampment and broke the back of Occupy.

Instead of changing the world, the Occupy movement fell apart. When I decided to re-issue *Occupy Space* in 2022, I changed the title to *BadAsstronauts* because no one even knew what Occupy referred to anymore. The movement that had given me so much hope back in 2011 had failed. The American space program stayed dead. Space travel became a playground for billionaires, the latest version of superyacht one-upmanship for one-percenters. The economy still felt shaky and the opioid crisis that started looking bad around 2011 had hollowed out the heartland by 2022. So few people believe in science today that anti-vaccination conspiracy theorists, who seemed like a marginal group back in 2011, dominate the national discourse. If things looked bad in 2011, they look even worse now. Hope may have been solely for suckers back then, but these days it feels like little more than an advertising slogan.

And yet...

The idea of a $15 minimum wage started with Occupy, and they made eliminating student debt part of the national conversation. The language about the ninety-nine percent versus the one percent feels like it's been around forever, but that came from Occupy, too.

People who got their feet wet with the Occupy movement went on to work in unions, the Bernie Sanders presidential campaign, and other activist organizations around the country. STEM has become the latest buzzword and backyard tinkerers are starting to shape the future. Rich Benoit built his own Tesla in the two-car garage underneath his house, an award-winning all-girl robotics team in Afghanistan designed a lower cost respirator using car parts during the first wave of the 2020 COVID-19 pandemic, and 14-year-old William Kamkwamba in Malawi jerry-rigged a wind turbine out of scrap metal to bring electric power to his village.

Things still feel drenched in despair, and yet I see small companies making compression suits at the Brooklyn Navy Yard and tiny labs designing open-source PPE to take the edge off the COVID crisis. For every person ranting about 5G chips in vaccines and stolen elections, I see people building the things they need, the things that help their neighbors, the things that open the door to the future, in their backyards, in their basements, in small workshops, not just in America but around the world.

Nothing depresses me more than footage of Jeff Bezos and Richard Branson shooting themselves into space. Nothing leaves me colder than a bunch of billionaires measuring their dicks. But it's only a matter of time before people start looking up at the stars and thinking, "Why not me?" And then they'll start tinkering in their backyards and their basements, they'll start crunching the calculations and reaching out to other people who feel the same way. They'll start pooling their spare time and their resources, matching their skills, sparking their torches, putting on their welding goggles, and when that happens it'll only be a matter of time. After all, going into space is just a problem and the thing about problems is they all come with solutions as long as we're willing to do the work. Why wait for someone else to take us to the stars? Why let someone else have all the fun? Why not do it ourselves?

After all, the sky belongs to everyone.

—Grady Hendrix
New York, NY
September 2021

ONE

Melville, South Carolina was out of money, it was out of jobs, it was out of hope, and today it was out of astronauts. It'd only had two to begin with, so it's not like there was a lot of room for error in the first place. One was Walter Reddie, a leftover from the Shuttle Program who couldn't even piss with conviction anymore. He was paunchy and pushing sixty, with bug eyes, a gray crew cut, and a face that was as ugly as a donkey's asshole. He wore his sagging ass and paunch down low like they were on worn-out suspenders, and the less said about his time in the Shuttle Program, the better.

The other astronaut was Walter Reddie's second cousin once removed, Bobby Campbell, Jr. He was twenty-nine years old and a flight engineer on Mission 31 to the International Space Station under Commander Paul Fields and right now he was all alone, 247 miles above the surface of the Earth, helplessly falling around the planet at 17,239 miles per hour with no way home. This had resulted in a crisis at Melville's Ron McNair High School.

"Everyone got off except him?" Mr. Gaudy, the headmaster, said to the NASA public relations officer who called him. "Every single other astronaut got off that space station except the one who was scheduled to speak at my graduation?"

"Would you like another astronaut?" the NASA official asked.

"By when?" Mr. Gaudy asked.

"End of the week."

"End of the week? That means I'll no longer have the use of our gymnasium. Melville is not made of stadium seating. I'll have to go to Gaffney and rent their AMC screen. Who's going to pay for that?"

"I could come and speak," the NASA official suggested.

"Are you an astronaut?"

"Public relations are a vital part of the American space program."

Mr. Gaudy terminated the conversation. No one wanted to hear what an almost-astronaut had to say. Just his luck that he had scheduled a graduation speaker who was one of those obnoxious martyr types, always looking for an opportunity to sacrifice himself for the "greater good" and play hero. Now Mr. Gaudy would have to make one of the most irritating phone calls of his entire life. He dialed Walter Reddie's number from memory.

"Walter, it's Glenn Gaudy over at the school."

"I knew you'd come crawling back," Walter slurred.

"I'm calling to see if you might want to speak at the graduation tomorrow?"

"Oh, yeah?"

"You've been the commencement speaker for so many years, I thought it would be special to have you do it again."

"Cause Bobby's stuck up in space. Haw, haw."

For ten years in a row, Walter Reddie had shown up loaded to the gills to give the graduation speech, and it was always the same. "Don't tell me the sky's the limit when there are footprints on the moon, follow your dreams, et cetera." Always delivered with a total lack of conviction and completely flammable breath.

Mr. Gaudy had been delirious with joy when he'd heard that Bobby Campbell, Jr. would be able to give the speech this year, and he'd lost no time in striking Walter Reddie from the program. But now here he was, back again. It was like the two of them were stuck in some kind of horrible marriage.

"What if I doan wanna do it?" Walter said, mush-mouthed.

Parents expected a commencement speaker and, more than that, they expected a celebrity. It was no good explaining to them that Ron McNair High School was too small to draw a celebrity worth the name. To them, explanations sounded like excuses, and excuses made them angry. Mr. Gaudy had no pride when it came to avoiding angry parents.

"I'll give you fifty dollars," he said.

"Sixty."

"I'll give you sixty dollars but no more. That's coming out of next year's textbook budget, so I hope you're happy. I'm drawing the line at sixty!"

Walter gave a phlegmy chuckle and hung up the phone. And that was how Mr. Gaudy wound up sitting on the portable stage in the Ron McNair High School gymnasium watching a sick and sweaty Walter Reddie staring at the deactivated scoreboard on the far wall as the high school string orchestra joylessly sawed its way through Pachelbel's Canon.

Mr. Gaudy found it troubling that Walter Reddie had arrived sober. He'd never seen the man sober in his life. But he had done the best he could with what the Lord had given him, and now there was no turning back.

The minutes limped by. Mr. Gaudy got up and gave his introduction, they droned through a hymn ("O God Our Help in Ages Past"), he introduced Walter Reddie, and then he prayed that nothing truly horrible would happen. As the smattering of applause died out, Mr. Gaudy was unnerved by Walter Reddie's steady stride to the podium but reassured when Reddie unfolded the same old greasy print-out he always used. Mr. Gaudy had seen Walter Reddie—cup of coffee in one hand, cigarette burning between his fingers—vomit explosively onto the school parking lot, then slur his way through this same speech without serious incident fifteen minutes later.

"Greetings, class of 2023," Walter began. "My name is Walter Reddie and I was an astronaut. Being an astronaut is hard work, but when you finally go into space, you realize it is work that matters. Think about this pale blue dot on which we all live. Do any of us ever expect to see it the way an astronaut does, looking at this tiny arena like a cosmic stage…"

Walter Reddie stopped. Carefully, he folded his speech up and tucked it back inside his jacket. He gripped the sides of the podium and lowered his head, like he was thinking hard. Mr. Gaudy did not like it when people thought hard. It never worked out well. Then Walter Reddie lifted his head and stared out at the forty-two kids fanning themselves in the humid gym.

"You're fucked," he said. Parents recoiled, kids pricked up their ears. "There ain't no jobs out there for you. They're all being hogged up by folks who want them worse. You're soft. You're weak. Most of you are borderline retarded, and I bet if you think real hard, you can't remember a single useful thing you've learned in the past twelve years you've spent cheating on tests, copying homework, playing video games, and huffing glue."

Mr. Gaudy was paralyzed with horror. It was like all his nightmares were coming true at the same time. A rambling drunken monologue he could have handled, but an attack on the American education system? And the insults! Plus the *r* word. These children were violent. Push them too far and they'd come at you with their phones. He'd had two teachers quit this year already because of what had been done to them on Instagram.

"My cousin is up there on the International Space Station," Walter Reddie said. "He stayed behind to manually undock the Soyuz reentry vehicles so his six crewmates could return safely to their families. He didn't give a tinker's damn that two of them were probably Putin-loving Russian spies and one was a godless Commie from Red China, because when times are tough, you don't see color.

"Now, NASA don't fly Space Shuttles no more, and the Commies crashed their last two Soyuz rockets, so everyone says that Bobby Junior is gonna be stuck up in space for a while. They say he won't die because Richard Branson is gonna build a space plane and go get him, but I'll tell you a fact: Richard Branson is a pussy. He comes from a long line of pussies born and raised in a country run by pussies who couldn't even beat a bunch of dirty, lowdown Nazis without our help. I'll tell you another fact. Bobby Junior is going to die up there because America has become a nation of people like you: cowards and fuck-tards who would rather send an email than go into space."

The graduating class of 2022 had never listened to a speech this long before. Normally, they'd be rioting by now, but Reddie's carefully timed insults had captured their attention. They had their phones out, recording his every word. It felt safer that way.

"When Bobby dies, that bloodless mummy in the White House is gonna make some pretty speeches and call him a hero and build him a monument and Bobby's momma will get a check in the mail and be invited to the Rose Garden so she can shake that grinning fuck's hand. But let me tell you something: she'd rather have her son back.

"So, I'm gonna do what the corporate knob-gobblers in the White House and the Commies in the Kremlin can't. I'm gonna do what those spineless nerds at NASA won't. I'm gonna build a rocket and I'm gonna bring my cousin back home to his momma. And the only reason I'm standing here today is because I need manpower. So do you, the future unemployed assholes and prison cell fillers of America, want to stand with me and do something with your miserable lives, or do you want to sit there and continue being incredible pussies like Richard Branson?"

There was silence. Then Jimmy Ferguson started laughing, a harsh, braying sound that echoed through the gym. Other students joined in, and soon Walter Reddie was being razzed by the entire graduating class. He flipped them the bird and someone threw a chair. He flinched but there wasn't enough power behind the throw and it crashed into the podium, which went over and landed on Mr. Gaudy's foot. Coach Greene stood up and began blowing his whistle. Someone tipped over the American flag. Chaos reigned.

The change had come over Walter Reddie in the middle of the night. He had been putting a hurting on a bottle of vodka when Glenn Gaudy called. Ever since his retirement, two activities took up his time. One was cashing his social security check, the other was hiding from the big clock. When the house was quiet, he heard it, ticking away the minutes of his life. He smoked like a chimney, he drank like a fish, and he had fourteen more years to kill? How many more hours of TV did he have to watch before he died? How many more newspapers did he have to read? How many more bullshit conversations did he have to have with the teller at the bank?

"Fuck all y'all!" he roared, opening his eighth mini-bottle of Popov. "Let's see you process this, you fucking piece-of-shit liver."

He'd woken up around three in the morning and stumbled out into his front yard to stare up at the stars. Normally they made him feel small, but tonight they just pissed him off. He was a failed astronaut. He'd spent the first half of his life training for something he'd never been allowed to do, and now he was spending the second half waiting to die. He knew what fucking was like, he'd done his drugs back in the Air Force, he had an ex-wife and a son who didn't talk to him, golf was for assholes, he'd fixed plenty of cars, so what the fuck was he supposed to do now?

"Fuck you, space!" he yelled. His voice sounded small.

He'd called Bobby Jr.'s momma, Gail, earlier that day and tried to reassure her that NASA would rescue Bobby Jr. soon, but he didn't actually believe those cowards would do a damn thing, and he was so drunk he'd spent most of the call cursing randomly. By the time he'd gotten off the phone, Gail was sobbing and her new husband (Kenny? Mark?) was yelling at him on the other extension. Now, standing in his front yard, Walter had what's known as a moment of clarity.

"Fuck NASA," he said out loud. "Want a thing done, you gotta do it your own goddamn self."

Then he passed out and crapped his pants.

Normally, he woke up the next morning with his drunken vows forgotten, but this one he remembered, probably because those were the last pair of jeans he owned without holes in them. He pounded this vow against the anvil of his brain in the shower, as he shaved, as he put on the one suit that still fit him in the waist, and by the time he was in his truck heading for the school, it was pure, incandescent rage. He'd even forgotten to have his breakfast beers.

Now, five days after the graduation debacle, he stood in front of his family out in the barn. Walter hated having people on his farm because it was an embarrassing wreck, but there had been no other offers to lend a hand, and so he'd used guilt against the only people who actually knew Bobby Jr., and now here they were, staring up at him like a bunch of cows chomping Cheetos. He'd told them it'd be a weekend-long family get-together. Some of them had come from as far as three hours away.

"I don't give a shit that y'all came," he began, inspirationally. "I'm going to get Bobby Junior down. Y'all wanna help, fine, but don't expect me to give out much in the way of *please* and *thank you*. We got a job to do, and we're going to do it. That's the American way. Now, how many of you are good at math?"

They just stared up at him with their big, dumb moon faces.

"Any of you studied engineering?"

One of the cousins from his daddy's side of the family raised his hand.

"I got a friend at work who knows engineering," Carl Suggs said.

"Where you work?"

"Wal-Mart."

"Can you get him out here?"

"He got fired for failing his piss test. I think he moved to Florida."

"Then shut your pie hole, Carl. Anyone else?"

Nothing but crickets.

"Look here," Walter said, trying a new tack. "How many of y'all went to college?"

"Community college count?" Cousin Jay asked.

"It's got *college* in the name, don't it?" Walter said.

Three hands went up out of twenty-two people.

"High school?"

Twelve more hands went up, including one from Norbert Sykes.

"Put your dern hand down, Norbert," Big Patty said. "You only graduated because you threatened to sue the school district for discrimination."

"Uh-unh," Norbert said. "I got that diploma fair and square whether the school give it to me or a court of law."

Walter picked up his folding metal chair and threw it against the prefab metal wall of his barn. Everyone jumped in terror, but at least they started paying attention again.

"I know what y'all're asking yourselves."

"Where's the beer?" Norbert asked, and everybody laughed.

"Y'all're asking yourselves how we're going to get Bobby Junior back home to Gail and all them when all we got is Walter and his busted-up farm. Well, to get Bobby Junior back, we got to go into outer space, but that ain't as hard as it sounds."

"Ain't easy, either," Uncle AJ said.

"A rocket's nothing but an explosion with a hole at one end and a man at the other," Walter said.

"You talking about a rocket or about your face?" Norbert quipped, getting some more cheap laughs.

"Settle down, Norbert," Uncle AJ said. "I'm not stupid, Walter. You may think you're superior to me because you sat in a rocket that didn't go nowhere a couple of times, but piss on that. I've been on roller coasters that took me closer to space than you ever been. And I know, and everyone in this room knows, that there ain't no way we're building no spaceship. NASA done it a bunch of times and it takes them billions of dollars and all kinds of special wrenches and robot arms and computers. See the people in this room? We're all here because we feel sorry for Gail, but as soon as you're done barking, we're all going to go on home and forget everything you ever said. I hate to put it that way, but it's the plain truth."

"You done, Uncle AJ?" Walter asked.

"Reckon so."

"Then you listen to me," Walter said. "We're not building a rocket to the moon, you dumb fuck. We're going into low Earth orbit, which is about a hundred miles straight up. I'm not pretending it's easy, but it ain't all it's cracked up to be, neither. Get that shit you've seen on the Discovery Channel right out of your minds. That's pure government propaganda.

"Now, I hate the Commies more than anyone, but they built their rockets right. Did you hear that word? Rockets. Not Space Shuttles. Not Branson space planes. Worst thing NASA ever did was build the Space Shuttle. Getting out of the gravity well puts forces on a machine so demonic, it twists their engines into pretzels and stresses steel until it's as brittle as glass. That's why the Apollo Program sent hundred-ton rockets up and only got seven-ton space capsules back. By the time them things reached orbit, ninety-three tons of them were about as usable as Great-Grandaddy Avery's dick."

"I'll remind you that there are ladies present," Uncle AJ warned.

"While our government was farting around building the Space Shuttle, the Commies were shooting ten times more rockets into space than we ever did. NASA spent all its time optimizing weight to payload, trying to get maximum efficiency. The Commies went for overkill: big fucking explosions that shot shit into the sky. It weren't pretty, but it worked.

"NASA built a Space Shuttle that you got to fly and land like a damn airplane. The Commies just let their shit fall back to Earth. Ballistics is the science of shit falling down, and we know a fuckton more about that than we do about flying. Crap's been falling down for millions of years, but we've only been flying for about a hundred. Figuring out where something's gonna land is a calculation even the most ass-backwards math student in the most underfunded shitstain of a high school can manage. But flying? You need a damn degree to figure that out.

"The Commies don't value human life the way we do. NASA got backups and backups and then some backups on the backups for their systems. They got redundancies for every eventuality. But the Commies? They just shoot fuckers up into space and they either live or they don't. They're the original orbital badasses. You know what they use as life pods on the International Space Station? The Soyuz. Not the goddamn Space Shuttle. Because the systems our country builds, God bless America, are fragile and neurotic compared to the pig-iron Commie death machines that come out of the USSR. So, we're going up into space the Commie way, not the Cape Canaveral way."

"I won't tolerate un-Americanism," Uncle AJ protested.

"You know what's un-American?" Walter snarled. "In Copenhagen, there are EU-worshipping, socialized-medicine-loving homosexuals in leather pants building a manned rocket in their spare time. If you're telling me that those bearded fucks can do something that good Americans like us can't, then I say you're the anti-American traitor who should be in a cell in Guantanamo Bay.

"Is there any of you who got the balls to tell me that we can't do this? Is there any of you who want to rise up and say, 'Yes, I am a Christ-hating enemy combatant who thinks we should piss on the ashes of our 9/11 dead'? Because if you are, I'll slay you where you stand as a terroristic waste of sperm."

No one had the balls.

"So, we're going to build two different machines," Walter said. "This is for you, Uncle AJ, who don't know the difference between a rocket and a spacecraft. We're gonna build a big-ass launch vehicle that'll get to escape velocity and put us into orbit. That's the rocket. Then we're gonna build a little bitty spacecraft that'll be strapped to its tip. When the launch vehicle's burned up all its fuel, it'll separate and fall back down to Earth, burning up in the atmosphere, while the space craft'll intercept the ISS's orbital trajectory, and the two of them'll nuzzle up like lovebirds. That's when we'll snag Bobby Junior, pull him on board, and then let our orbit decay until we drop back down to Earth, and return him to the tender ministrations of Gail. Any questions?"

Silence. People cut their eyes to their neighbors to see if it made sense to them.

"Did y'all understand a single word that's come out of my mouth since I asked about your high school diplomas?"

There was a weak chorus of *no*s. For the first time since getting this idea, Walter Reddie despaired. He was just about to throw another chair at the wall, when a little voice piped up from the door.

"Excuse me, is this where y'all're building the rocket ship?"

The barn filled with the *shss*ing sound of twenty-one denim-clad butts and one butt wrapped in polyester rotating on chairs as everyone turned to stare at Tiara Flynn, hovering in the doorway. She was seventeen years old and she looked she'd wandered in from a toddler's beauty pageant. Less than five feet tall with the makeup and nails of Whitney Houston, wearing big body curls that she'd lacquered with too much product, wearing a jewel pink hoodie and a pair of shorts made for a chihuahua, it seemed clear to everyone that all her taste was in her mouth.

"Strip club's down the road a ways, darlin'," Walter snarled.

Instantly, Tiara's eyes turned bright red and soaking wet.

"You don't speak to a girl that way," Big Patty said, trying to heave herself up out of her chair. "You can be mean to us 'cause we're your family. But this girl is a stranger and you're making us look like trash when you talk that way."

"I just came to help," Tiara said. "Heard about you at graduation and thought I'd come see what was up."

"Now you seen," Walter Reddie said. "So git."

"Well, fuck you, too," Tiara said, running out the door as mascara streaked down her cheeks.

"Damn, Walt, that was cold," Carl Suggs said. "I used to date that girl. She's nice."

"I don't know why you're defending her," Uncle AJ said to Carl. "She got you to pay for her A&P license and then dumped your ass. It was embarrassing."

Walter Reddie's ears pricked up.

"She got her A&P license?"

"It belongs to Carl," Big Patty said. "He paid for the damn thing."

Walter Reddie sprinted past all their astonished faces and out into the dirt drive. Over by the house where all the cars were parked he saw Tiara getting into her Hyundai. He tried to speed up but he was already out of breath.

"Wait!" he wheezed.

He hopped the fence and managed to catch his ankle on the top rail and go facedown in the dirt. He picked himself up and limped to her car as fast as he could. She tried to run him over.

"You got your A&P license?" he shouted through the windshield, bracing both hands against the hood while trying to keep her overgrown Japanese lawnmower from running him down.

"Fuck you!" she shrieked, barely audible over the sound of her high-pitched engine revving.

"Please," he shouted, and dropped to his knees in front of her car. "Do you really have your A&P license?"

She rolled down the driver's side window.

"Carl better not be talking trash about me."

"He only said good things," Walter lied. He clasped his hands, as if he was in prayer, and knee-walked towards her open window. It hurt like hell. "You saw what I have to work with. I need an airframe-and-powerplant tech like I need the love of God."

"I..." she started, then she turned off her engine. "I quit one month shy of graduating. They shut down the Boeing plant and I didn't see the use."

She rested her forehead on the steering wheel and let her tears flow. Walter Reddie stood up and looked at this tiny girl, barely bigger than a large toddler, and rifled through his mind, trying to remember what to do next. Tentatively, he put one hand on her shoulder. That seemed to go okay. He patted it.

"There, there," he said. "That's a two-year program. That makes you twenty-three months smarter than every other moron in that room. Now stop crying and let me show you what a launch vehicle looks like."

It's not as easy as you might think to build a three-stage, eight-hundred-ton rocket in your backyard. Walter Reddie was learning that lesson firsthand.

"NASA spends a hundred billion dollars every year on this," Tiara said.

"I got certain advantages over NASA," Walter said.

"Like what?"

"Like I don't give a shit if I die."

It was true. NASA wanted to build safe, efficient, reusable space systems with multiple redundancies. Walter just wanted to strap himself to a rocket and shoot it into the sky, and if he died, that was merely Jesus's way of saying it was time to come home.

"Redundancies are for sissies," he said. "And we'll all probably go to prison for doing this, so *reusable* is the least of my worries."

"Oh," Tiara said. She got sad and serious. "I can't go to prison. I got a daughter."

"Don't worry about that," Walter said. "Chances are good we'll blow ourselves up before things even get to that point."

That didn't much cheer her up.

"So, what's the plan?" she asked Walter.

"The way I figure it, we got about six months before Bobby Junior dies. First thing we need to do is get word to him that we're coming, keep him from doing something stupid like killing himself."

"Why would he do that?"

"Space is a lonely, godless place. He might choose to gulp some morphine and vent himself out the airlock rather than starve to death. If he knows that his people are down here working towards getting him home, he'll hang on. Who you know that does ham radio?"

And that's how they got Jimmy Royal involved in this mess. He'd lost both his legs from the knees down when a tank ran over them in Vietnam. He'd returned stateside, given up drinking, took up baby-making, and got hooked on ham radio. Six boys, three girls, and one exhausted, long-suffering wife with a Christ-like disposition later, he had a thriving wireless-repair business and the most sophisticated ham gear money could buy. Tiara had met him while doing community outreach for her church.

"What do you say, Jimmy?" Walter asked. "We talk to Bobby Junior and maybe his momma will get a few words through to keep his morale up?"

"Sounds like the Christian thing to do," Jimmy Royal said. "I'll need to know the frequency, and you'll need someone to calculate when he'll be overhead, and I'll need fifty dollars."

"What's the fifty dollars for?"

"I don't run a charity," Jimmy Royal said. "You want a man to do a job, you pay a man his value."

Calculating the orbit could be a teachable moment, Walter figured, so he forked over the cash, then went home and examined his relatives for mathematical aptitude. He noticed that whereas most of them were outside playing touch football, drinking his beer at the kitchen table, or watching TV, Big Patty was absorbed in *The Big Book of Sudoku*, so she became his first candidate.

"Astrophysics really ain't much harder than doing your bills," Walter told her.

That turned out to be a lie. He and Big Patty fought all night. Walter liked to pass on knowledge via shouting.

Big Patty was a poor student and she responded to the pressure by screaming back at him and throwing the one 1979 physics textbook Walter had across the room. At a little after 2 AM, even Tiara gave up and drove home, figuring that by now Bathsheba would be fast asleep and she could catch a few hours of rest before morning.

Around 5 AM, things between Walter and Big Patty came to a head. After threatening to shove the textbook up his "flat Reddie ass," Big Patty snatched up her pencil in a rage and jammed some numbers down on her legal pad.

"If he was there on the map about three days ago, then he's going to be overhead here Tuesday at 6:33 PM," she said. "Now the hell with you. I'm going to bed."

Walter opened up his laptop, went to the orbital tracker website, and double-checked.

"Yep," he said. "You're right on the money."

"You had it online this whole time?" she asked.

"You got to start learning orbital mechanics sometime. Before I'm done with you, your brain's gonna be as big as your ass."

Big Patty wasn't pleased, but she kind of was at the same time.

It took Jimmy Royal a few days to hit the exact ten-minute window when the ISS was directly overhead, and he was able to have a confused conversation with Bobby Junior. He called Walter, who brought Big Patty and all the rest over.

"I figure for fifty dollars, the least I could do is record it for posterity," Jimmy Royal said, hitting the space bar on his keyboard.

"International Space Station, this is Melville, South Carolina calling. Do you read me, over? International Space Station, this is Melville, South Carolina calling. Do you read me, over?"

"Melville, SC, this is International Space Station. Who's this? Over."

"This is Jimmy Royal from up on Route 11, by the All-U-Eat Chicken Barn. Over."

"Mr. Royal, this is Bobby Campbell Junior. It is good to hear your voice, sir. Over."

"I've been told that I need to get a message to you, over. Are you reading me, Bobby? Over."

"Tell my mom—" Bobby began, and then his voice broke.

"Simmer down," Jimmy's recorded voice said. "I've got a message to read you. It says stand by. We're bringing you home. Over."

"NASA's been talking to you?" Bobby's voice was full of excitement. "They're coming to get me? Over."

"They're not coming to get you. *We're* coming to get you. Over."

"Come again, Melville. Can you repeat? Over."

"We're coming to get you," Jimmy said. "Over."

"Who's *we*? Over."

"Well, your cousin Walter Reddie seems to be leading the effort. Over."

Carl Suggs gave Walter a thumbs-up and a big grin, while Big Patty patted Walter on the back. He was being talked about in space.

"They're sending Walter up here? I don't follow. Can you clarify? Over."

"He's building himself a rocket, son, and he's coming up into space to get you home. Over."

There was a long silence. Very long.

"You still there, Bobby? Over," Jimmy said.

"I'm passing out of the window," Bobby said. "Tell my mom that I love her, and tell Diane—"

"Don't give up, son," Jimmy shouted on the recording. "Your cousin's coming to fetch you home, over. Bobby? Bobby, do you read me? Over."

"And that's all she wrote," Jimmy said, hitting the Stop button on his keyboard.

People looked around at each other, grinning like fools. Making contact with Bobby Campbell, Jr. up in space made it feel real. They were going to do this.

"You got any beer in this place?" Uncle AJ asked. "I feel like a celebration is in order."

"That's going to be $1.25 for the recording," Jimmy said to Walter as general revelry broke out all around them. "I don't do freebies. Even for Carolina astronauts."

* * *

That night, back at the farm, everyone buzzed on Coors Light, Walter finally had the talk with his family that he'd been dreading.

"We're going to need money to do this," he said. "No question. I'm going in to Melville Trust tomorrow morning, first thing, and I'm putting a mortgage on this place. I expect y'all to do the same."

"We can't put a mortgage on your place," Norbert called out.

"Don't be thick, Norbert," Walter said. "All your houses, all your property, all your deposits, whatever it is, we need to turn it into cash."

They just stared at him, beers forgotten in their hands.

"Y'all heard Bobby Junior on that recording," he snapped. "Y'all heard how alone he is up there in that big empty sky. Can any of you look Gail in the eye and tell her you didn't do everything in your power to bring her son home? Can any of you go to her and say, 'Well, we're real sorry, Gail; we wanted to bring Bobby Junior home but it just cost too much money'?"

They weren't buying it.

"This is like a rocket. You know how you burn everything in stage one and then it falls off and burns up in the atmosphere, and then you burn everything in stage two, and it falls off and burns up in the atmosphere, and finally you get where you're going."

They didn't.

"You need to turn your property into money, and we need to burn that money up so we can get into space and rescue Bobby Junior."

A few nods, some muttered words. They got it, but they didn't like it. Well, there wasn't much he could do about that, Walter reckoned. But the one thing he did know was that he had unleashed the most powerful force in a family: shame. He was shaming them, and there was nothing more likely to wring cash out of their chicken necks and beer bellies than shame. They might moan and groan, but at the end of the day, he knew that none of them could face Gail with a guilty conscience.

He decided to take a sleeping pill—what he called three mini-bottles of Popov—to his room and turn in early. Tomorrow he had the grim privilege of visiting his bank and turning everything he owned on God's green earth into cash. Then he had to come home and try to teach his family the equations they needed to start working out how to get into low Earth orbit.

Next morning, Walter Reddie came outside with a furry, hung-over head to find that cars were leaving. Tiara was sitting in a busted-out lawn chair on his porch with tears running down her face. In his big back yard, SUVs and Honda Accords and minivans were turning his grass into mud, circling around and pulling out the gate and onto the road that led to the highway.

"Where's everyone going?" he asked Tiara, genuinely confused.

"They're leaving, Walter," she said, looking up at him with watery eyes. "They're going home."

"Why?" was all he could think to say.

"They talked until late last night, and they don't think you can do it."

"They don't think I can do it?" he repeated, dully.

"They aren't up for it," Tiara said.

"Aren't up for it?" he said, outraged. He ran at Norbert's minivan and slapped on the window until Norbert braked and rolled it down.

"Where the hell're you going, 'bert?"

"We all want Bobby home, like you do," Norbert said. "But this is a crazy thing, Walter. We can't risk everything we got just on your say-so. If you had a man from NASA here, maybe everyone'd stay, but you don't even have that."

"We got to hang together," Walter said. "If this is going to work, we got to hang together. We can do this."

"You know how people say 'It ain't rocket science'? Well, this *is* rocket science. How do you expect us to do all this, Walter?"

"Aren't you tired of always being small?" Walter Reddie asked.

But Norbert just gave him a look of disgusted pity,

then he rolled up his window and bumped on out of the yard. His was the last minivan in the caravan heading due east out of Melville.

A giant black hole of despair formed in Walter's chest, and it started sucking him down before he plugged it up with rage. Anger was the only weapon he had left; it was the only thing that was keeping him going. It didn't matter if there was nobody left on the farm. It didn't matter if his entire family had abandoned him. Walter had been abandoned before. He'd been abandoned by professionals. Watching the butt ends of his family's beaters and minivans disappear down the dirt road towards the highway, Walter didn't allow himself to feel anything but incandescent rage.

"We're going to do this," he said out loud.

Tiara didn't reply.

"All that poor white trash running away means that this is a good idea. Those shitkickers have run away from every opportunity in their lives. We're better off without them."

"I guess so…" Tiara said.

Walter turned around.

"The fuck is your problem? I said we're going to do this and that means we're going to do this. I'm an astronaut, goddammit!"

"I Googled you," Tiara said, and she looked down quickly.

Walter paused like he'd been slapped in the face.

"Oh," he said.

Walter could only imagine what his career looked like on Google without him there to sort of explain things and show why they weren't as bad as they looked. The closest he'd ever come to space was sitting in the *Discovery* for three hours before his mission was scrubbed. Twice.

The second time, he'd reported errors in two of the four avionics processors, and that had led to the mission being grounded. The likelihood of half the processors going kablooey all at the same time was slim, and so some people had started going behind his back and saying that he'd made up those errors or done them himself. They said he'd faked it and cost NASA millions of dollars because he was scared of going into space. They called him a Launchpad Pussy. True or not, the only thing he'd been allowed to fly after that was a desk. That would look pretty poorly on Google.

"You going to take off too?" he asked. He could afford to ask blunt questions like this. He had plenty of vodka in the house.

Tiara shook her head.

"Why the fuck not?"

"I don't know," she whispered. "Nothing else to do."

"Go see a movie," Walter said. "Meet a boy. Get a job at Wal-Mart."

And Tiara almost told him. She almost told him that she had her whole life stretched out in front of her and it looked like her momma's and it made her want to scream. She almost told him that she had only ever had one dream and it was that one day she'd take Bathsheba to Orlando, Florida to see Disney World in a plane she'd built.

She had imagined the whole thing right down to their matching outfits and how they'd be sitting in an even-numbered row, aisle and window seats, and Tiara would point out the window at the engines and say to Sheba, "See those? That's what makes the plane fly. Mommy built those."

And she'd imagined passing on to her princess, like a sacred trust, the knowledge that her mommy could build high-bypass turbojet engines. Everything would have been different for Tiara if she'd known her mom had been capable of doing something besides drinking wine and getting knocked up and knocked down by a string of assholes who never stayed.

And she almost said that, she almost told Walter because she felt like he was the same way, but then she looked into his pissed-off, bloodshot redneck eyes and she knew that if she said that, he was going to say something awful because he'd wanted the same thing five thousand disappointments ago. He'd wanted to build something that he could point to and be proud of and instead he'd spent twenty years at NASA filling out paperwork and now all he had left was being nasty and drunk.

"I just don't want to be scanning barcodes for the rest of my life," she finally said. "You know what I mean?"

"Yeah," Walter said. "I do."

There was an awkward silence, and the two of them just stood there for a while because there was really nothing else left to say.

Walter had intended to go upstairs and get royally drunk, just to really pull the dirt down over his head, but once he got up there, he looked out his bedroom window and saw that Tiara's Hyundai was still in the driveway and having someone else in the house took the joy out of being miserable. He sulked around for a few hours, drank some vodka, and listened to the ticking of the big clock until he was crawling out of his skin. When he came downstairs, Tiara was hunched over his kitchen table, deep in some calculations.

"Hey—" he said.

"You gave me a heart attack!" she shouted. "I was… I started working, but I needed some scrap paper, and you had these printouts and I used them. But I only got through half the formulas…"

Walter looked at page after page of densely packed numbers and calculations. Did her boyfriends have any idea of what kind of brain was hiding underneath all that makeup?

"Looks all right," he said.

"I didn't know how to find things like the mean weight of the launch vehicle or what kind of propellant you wanted to use, so I had to make some guesses. I hope that's okay?"

"This ain't enough," he said.

"I'm sorry."

"It's not you," he said. "Norbert may be the laziest man in five counties, but he was right about one thing: this *is* rocket science. We need a rocket scientist."

"I don't know any," she apologized.

"Me neither," Walter said. "Grab your gear. We're going to Rocket City."

Tiara worked on her math for the entire three-hundred-and-twenty-one-mile trip to Huntsville, Alabama. When they crossed the state line into Georgia, she was floundering, but by the time they entered Alabama, she was as focused as a laser, picking absently at her eyebrows and correcting her own mistakes, pen flying over the paper.

That night, Walter made the rounds of Huntsville, and early the next morning, they arrived at the brick rancher out in the suburbs. No one answered the front door, so Walter jimmied the latch on a wooden gate and they went around to the backyard. Through the windows of the Florida room they could see a long, gaunt man with a skinny, unshaved chicken neck lying on a lounge chair like a corpse, half-buried in newspapers. He was wearing gray sweats. Walter banged on the glass with the flat of his hand. The man sat up like he'd been caught doing something.

"Go away," he shouted through the glass.

"Paul Rawe?" Walter shouted back.

"No," the man said, and then he scrambled out from under his pile of newspaper and disappeared into the house.

Walter tried the door. It was open.

"Paul Rawe," he called, entering the house.

"Don't shoot us," Tiara squeaked. "Please?"

The man stood in the doorway to the dining room and looked at them incredulously. In one hand was a wooden kitchen spoon.

"Are you inside my house?" he asked. "This state has castle doctrine, you know."

"You're Paul Rawe, the unemployed rocket scientist?" Walter asked.

"Who?" the man asked, blinking. "What? Who told you that?"

"A fellow I met at the bar last night said I should talk to his brother who worked at the Wal-Mart and he said that I needed to speak with a gal whose son was married to a fellow who told me that his sister was best friends with a hairdresser who sent me to her husband who happens to be your dentist and he told me where you lived and said that you're an out-of-work rocket scientist.

"Hi," Tiara said.

"Propulsion engineer," the pale man said, blinking rapidly. "I'm a propulsion engineer. Am I in trouble?"

"We're building a rocket down in Melville, South Carolina," Walter said. "And we could use a good propulsion engineer."

"You're home invaders. I'm going to call the police if you don't leave."

Walter was very good at ignoring people who wanted him to do something.

"I heard about the Constellation program getting shut down, Walter said. "And then I read about most of the Marshall Space Flight Center getting cut, so I figured Huntsville would be full of out-of-work rocket scientists. I also figured that after sucking off the government teat for most of their lives, all those brainiacs might suddenly find themselves real hungry when the Feds put their bra back on. Figured that might make one of them more willing to help me build my rocket."

"I'm sorry," Paul said to Tiara. "Please remove your friend from my home."

"I don't think I can," Tiara said. "He's real hard to remove."

"I don't understand any of this," Paul Rawe said.

"Me build rocket. You help," Walter said.

Just then, the front door opened.

"Paul? Whose car is that?" a feminine voice said, and then a beautiful redhead, younger than Paul by about a decade, shimmered into the room. She had some lipstick on her front teeth and the kind of curves packed into the kind of tight dress that got men stabbed with broken bottles in bars. "Why do you have a spoon?"

"Self-defense," he said. "They just came in."

"Why didn't you call the police?"

"We didn't break in," Walter said. "The door was wide open."

"The back door!" Paul said. "They want me to come to South Carolina and build a rocket with them. Call 9-1-1."

"Why?" she asked. "If that's all they want, I think it sounds like a terrific idea."

"But they're home invaders," Paul said.

"Lynne Rawe," the woman said, shaking Walter and Tiara's hands. "I'm sorry you're here to see him like this, but it's probably for the best. Do you know where I just was, Paul?"

"Honey, these people need to leave," Paul whined.

"I was talking to a lawyer. Do you know what he was doing?"

"Honey…" Paul whined.

"He was telling me my options regarding divorce."

"Not in front of strangers!" Paul said.

"Why?" Lynne asked. "You sit around, playing on the computer all day. You read three different newspapers with the same news in them every morning. Who even reads newspapers anymore? It's sick. Every time I come home, I figure I'm going to find you hanging from your belt with some note blaming everyone else pinned to your shirt. I was going to leave you, but I'll give you some time to change if you think this rocket project can get you out of your rut."

Paul looked crushed. He sat down on an ottoman.

"Go build your giant phallic symbol. We need some time apart. When you come back, maybe we can work something out. But I can't live with a man who wears the same sweatpants every day. I just can't."

Paul had tears running down his face, but he was clearly not good at articulating his feelings, so he didn't reply. Instead, he turned to Walter and Tiara.

"I can only commit to examining how far you've gotten and perhaps giving you some pointers."

"Whatever you want," Walter said.

"Come by here tomorrow morning around 7 AM, and we can head to South Carolina and you can show me what you've got."

They let themselves out.

They didn't get to Walter's farm until three PM. Paul spent most of the ride crying quietly in the back seat and downing Mountain Dews. He was so caffeinated by the time they arrived that they went right to the barn. Walter slid open the doors with a flourish to reveal: nothing. There were tools hanging on the right-hand wall, folding chairs stacked up beneath them, and a whiteboard on the left where he'd tried to teach his family the basics of rocketry, but most of the barn was taken up by empty air.

"Where's the rocket?" Paul asked.

"We haven't gotten that far," Walter said.

Paul's face went slack and sad. Walter decided to remind him of the higher purpose to which he aspired.

"How long did your wife want you to be gone?" he asked. "Cause I got a spare room if you need to be away for a week or two, make her think you're manning up."

Paul cleared his throat.

"I prefer it this way," he said. "No bad habits. A clean slate so we can build an optimal launch system. Perfect. Good. Good, good, good."

That night, Paul planted a paper seed in the barn that grew into a jungle as he began to work out the calculations they needed to build their rocket. Tiara brought a playpen out for Bathsheba because her mama was dating again and couldn't look after her anymore. To the steady sounds of her daughter moping and sighing in her sleep, the two of them started working equations. Day after day, the papers grew until they covered three folding tables, and then they spread up the walls. Maps, printouts, color photos, papers taped to papers taped to papers, creeping towards the ceiling like kudzu.

Two weeks after Paul arrived, Tiara called some pyro buddies from her old class and they showed up in a primer-dotted Chevy Malibu hauling a customized horse trailer.

"Rocket-car racing isn't technically, um, legal?" the least pimply of the three explained. "But we've been working on an engine anyways. Don't tell?"

They opened up the horse trailer to reveal a huge pile of bubble wrap and packing tape. The three of them—Shawn, Natty L (for Natural Light, his favorite beer) and Abraham—hauled it out of their trailer on a floor jack and dragged it down a ramp made of scrap metal, leaving it sinking into Walter's dirt yard. Natty L clawed the bubble wrap off and the powerful, ugly hunk of metal sat revealed in the afternoon sun. Paul walked around it, nervously blinking like a baby bird.

"I'm sorry," he finally said. "But it's going to have to be totally rebuilt."

"Cool," Natty L said. "Show us how?"

"It's a time-intensive project," Paul said.

"The only one of us who has a job is Abe, and he's just temping. You're a NASA scientist. It'll be educational or something."

And so the Three Pyros moved into the barn, pushing the parts catalogs and printouts and reams of blank paper and Sharpies and index cards and baby toys to one side and throwing down sleeping bags patched with duct tape on the other. From then on, if you were working in the barn, you had to make sure one of the doors was open or you'd suffocate on the smell of diapers and unwashed teenaged boy.

Paul spent all of his time working with Tiara, leaving it to her to communicate his needs to the Three Pyros. It wasn't just that he found their adolescent enthusiasm intimidating, but he was also spending every moment he could steal from the project huddled over his cell phone, hidden in some far-off corner of Walt's property, having whispered, urgent conversations with his wife, trying to save his marriage. Tiara was either working on the basic plans for the launch vehicle and the spacecraft, or changing Bathsheba's diapers. Walter spent most of his time making sure people got fed and protecting his property from dangerous vodka build-ups.

As the plans began to take shape and the first month rolled by on the calendar, Paul and Walter had a frank conversation.

"We need to start cutting steel and building this shit or everyone's going to go home," Walter said, leaning against the fence where he'd cornered Paul, interrupting one of his secret conversations.

"I don't… I don't know if that's a good idea," Paul said. "I have some preliminary designs, but we need further testing before we actualize them."

"Testing is for NASA," Walter said. "We're American. We build shit."

"Well, before we do that, we need some more people."

"Done."

The next morning, six hobby flyers showed up.

"Southeastern Rocket Racing team," the youngest of them announced. "We saw a post on a rocketry Discord channel and came to see what's up."

Rocket Racing was supposed to be a new arm of NASCAR that raced low-altitude rocket planes and made billions of dollars, but the startup costs were so prohibitive that the only results the league had to show for itself were a bunch of regional teams that never made it past the "fly and die" testing stage. All Walter had to do was chum the water, dangling the bait that a real live rocket was actually getting built by a real live (former) NASA propulsion engineer, and frustrated rocket-racing enthusiasts started showing up at the farm.

"These are real interesting," one of them said, after Tiara and Paul stammered and stuttered and mumbled their way through a show-and-tell of the basic blueprints. "You mind if we come out here again next weekend and help out some?"

"Come on down," Walter said.

So they did. And they told friends, who told friends, who posted to Facebook, who put it on Twitter, who uploaded it to their blogs, who linked it to Reddit. And people started to arrive. Three weeks later, Walter was ready to make a second broadcast to Bobby Junior. He got Jimmy Royal to set it up live.

"ISS, this is Melville, SC, do you read me? Over."

"Come in, Melville; this is ISS. Over."

"Bobby, this is Walter Reddie. Over."

"Hey, Walter. Jimmy told me you wanted to fly up here and see me. I'll trade places with you if you want, over."

"Bobby, I want you to believe what I'm saying to you: hang on tight. We are building a rocket. We are going to get you down. This is real. It's happening. We're coming to bring you home."

The first dollar was the most important one. Later, they'd use the first $100 to buy a server they needed, they'd use the first $1000 to buy some Army Surplus tents, and they'd use the first $5000 to rent Port-a-Potties. When they hit their first $10,000, they'd start buying serious parts: steel plates, rods of polyurethane, metal grinders, and welding machines. They'd use the first $30,000 to buy tungsten-copper gas vanes, and when the donations reached $100,000, they'd use it to buy military-grade nozzles for the engine they were building. At the $150,000 mark, they'd start seriously tackling their cryogenic fuel storage tank.

But the first dollar was the one they all remembered. No one's sure how he heard about it—although Tiara thought it was because he and Walter had both been astronauts—but it came from Mike Mullane. It was just one dollar, which Walter sort of thought was a "fuck you," but no one else cared. What they cared about was that Mike Mullane, who'd logged three hundred and fifty-six hours in space on three separate Shuttle missions, knew about them. What they cared about was the note that came attached to his PayPal donation.

"*Your dreams should be bigger than you are. Godspeed—Mike.*"

They printed it out and it went up over the door of the barn with the dollar taped to it. Natty L tweeted a picture of it and the floodgates opened. Within a week, they had to assign three people to the website. By the time it was all over, twenty-four people were working on it full-time, managing PayPal donations, GoFundMe, and their Kickstarter campaign. If they had paid salaries, they would have been the biggest employer in Melville.

But the money was just fuel for the work, and the work was what mattered. Presided over by Paul and Tiara, they migrated from sketches and scribbles to blueprints. From blueprints to models, from models to testing. Everything was documented online, rocket forums critiqued their choices, and a node of the internet hive mind coalesced around their backwater site. It grew. It evolved.

Math majors in Japan checked their calculations, physicists in France helped with their launch trajectory (after suggesting that they were perhaps morons for not launching closer to the equator). Number junkies (some of whom Paul suspected weren't quite out of middle school) tweaked their delta-*v* budget, flame wars broke out over velocity optimization, a subreddit opened up about their project where insults were hurled by people who strongly felt they should move to a liquid engine rather than a solid-liquid hybrid.

Real people began to flood the farm, mostly weekend warriors with good tools and a tendency to injure themselves. They'd heard about it online, they'd seen stories about it on the news, usually buried way back in the human-interest section right before stories about puppies who could bark "God Bless America" and newts who did geometry. Their numbers grew outcast by weirdo by outcast: six kids from a Boy Scout troop who'd been suspended from school after their homebrewed nitro-burning funny car had exploded and put two teachers in the hospital, a one-eyed amateur astronomer from Hawaii who couldn't find work anyplace, a little person named Grekky who seemed to know an awful lot about wiring, a pair of registered nurses from Cleveland who were relentlessly upbeat no matter how many broken fingers, torn rotator cuffs, and burns they treated.

By the time his family showed back up, tails between their legs, Walt was too busy managing people to hold a grudge.

"I think you got the wrong impression before," Norbert said over beers at the kitchen table. "We support you, no matter what other people say."

"You support me?"

"We're your blood, cuz. Also, Big Patty didn't like that you said we were a bunch of sorry-ass white trash on that news story."

"Fine," Walter said. "I need janitors."

They settled on the term *Support Crew*, but it was basically the same thing. The twenty-two members of his family became the garbage cops, cleaning up trash, arranging to have the Port-a-Potties pumped, assigning sleeping areas as the crowds grew, as more and more people stayed, as the tents began their unstoppable spread across the back pasture. Fortunately, summer was coming, so being outside wasn't likely to result in anyone freezing to death.

The farm began to look like a tent city. They'd staked out a path from the new barn to where they were going to build the launchpad, and Uncle AJ took it upon himself to keep it clear, but every other open patch of ground filled up with tents and cars and caravans, RVs and mobile homes and trailers. Blue plastic tarps, camouflage ground cloths, backpacks, clotheslines, and folding tables. The crowd grew. And they kept coming.

Speed freaks at the end of their rope and looking for purpose came, reckless thrill-seekers who were in it for the velocity, show-offs and vacationing high school science teams, employees from bankrupt companies that never won the XPRIZE, and most of all the unemployed. Every day there were more of them. Machinists and makers and tool fabricators and shop stewards, assembly-line welders and scuba divers and conduit threaders and concrete finishers and cable strippers, linemen and firemen, vets who couldn't find jobs but knew Doppler radar, teenagers obsessed with cars but slaving at McDonald's, dropouts and overachievers and hydraulic engineers of all flavors.

Paul came out of his depression and put out a call to Huntsville, and a supply line opened up that turned into an all-out brain drain. A hierarchy formed. Around Paul, there was a cadre of the extremely technically gifted, the people who would do the thinking and figuring, and Tiara was the one they turned to when Paul wasn't there. She still wore so much perfume, you could smell her entering a room before you saw her, but she had a gift for solving thorny engineering problems, and the fact that she was more woman than most of these nerds had ever seen in their lives meant that they fell all over themselves trying to keep her happy.

Then there was a level of people who were technically skilled but weren't rocket scientists. These were the people who could take a big equation that'd been broken down into one hundred steps and tackle it, each of them crunching his or her own section and passing it to the next person, a living human computer. They called themselves the Big Brains. Then there were the great unwashed, the people who showed up without skills or talents, drawn by the fact that this was the only place in the Southeast where something real seemed to be happening. They called themselves the Rocket Zombies. The horde. The mass of people who, given the tools from the Big Brains, could accomplish anything through sheer force of numbers. If the Big Brains were the central nervous system, then the Rocket Zombies were the muscle. The Big Brains built the lever; the Rocket Zombies moved the world.

Eventually, the high school kids showed up, the ones who had hassled Walter at graduation. Walt decided to speak to them directly.

"Finally got tired of doing nothing with your lives?" he asked.

It was blunt and honest in a way that only the ones who had alcoholic parents were familiar with. It forced the kids to be direct in return.

"Yes, sir," Jimmy Ferguson said.

"Then go out to Memomma and get yourselves some work. I'm not giving out free hugs, I need your sweat and your pain and your blood."

Memomma was Walter's great-aunt, and she'd been put in charge of the jobs office, keeping track of who knew how to solder circuitry and who could find their way around a machine press. She kept it all in a giant Excel document that had become so massive, it took six minutes to load.

She also knew her way around kids, having had seven of them herself, and so she placed this sudden influx of high-schoolers under the supervision of an unemployed cement mason from Wisconsin who had been tasked with building the launchpad and the approach ramp. It was hard work, the kind that broke down egos and shattered bad attitudes. It was just what they needed.

It was also a disaster. The launchpad and the approach ramp came together more by accident than by design. The pathway from the fabrication hangar to the launchpad was staked off first, and that took two days. Then they needed cement. Wal-Mart was raided, then Lowe's, and finally Home Depot.

What they wound up with was a bunch of different brands of concrete all bought at retail and none of it very good. Two members of the football team even bought a twenty-pound bag of Quikrete and mixed it in. The concrete was poured, but they had prepared the sub base inconsistently and it started to crack even before it was dry as it all settled at different speeds.

To make it worse, they ran out of concrete before the project was even halfway finished, and it took them three days to find enough to complete it. The result was an approach ramp and launchpad that were an uneven patchwork of problems.

When it was finally completed, after two weeks of back-breaking labor, the concrete mason looked at the maze of crazing, cracks, and pop-outs and demanded that everyone break out the sledgehammers, bust it up, and start all over again.

It was the first time Walter was confronted with the need for procurement.

"I don't mean to be a worrywart," Paul said. "But this wasn't optimally executed because there was no coordination on the purchasing side. There will come a time when we'll need to negotiate the purchase of almost five hundred and fifty hundred thousand tons of liquid oxygen. We'll have to arrange delivery. We'll have to arrange payment. It will be an enormously complicated task, and the number of issues involved with a project as minor as the launchpad does not inspire much confidence."

Walter turned to Memomma and asked her who to talk to, and she steered him right to Miss Fisher and Miss Adele, two widows who lived about a mile from each other, both of whom were devotees of extreme couponing. He and Big Patty drove to their houses and appealed to the two women's competitive instincts.

The next morning, they showed up in hats and gloves, clutching alligator purses. They sat down at opposite ends of a folding table in the front room of Walter's house and began to fight to the death over who could get the best deals on pork and beans, toilet paper, hex wrench sets, and WeldPrint analyzers.

They got the Rocket Zombies to throw out all of Walter's furniture and put in metal shelving, and opened up a mutual stockpile in the living room that grew to consume the front porch, the hallways, the front room, the downstairs bathroom, and the attic. Eventually, they moved on to buying bigger and more complex items and scoring even more obscene discounts. When it came time to negotiate the purchase of military-grade copper-tungsten gas vanes, the Chinese never knew what hit them.

A bunch of Occupy types came and set up their own sector of camp where those in need of inspirational political analysis could go and get jacked up on ideology in the mornings before work began. They also concocted some badass cold-brew coffee in what looked like a giant chemistry set, and they seemed to have an unlimited supply of caffeine and class consciousness. Over the entrance to what became known as Camp Coffee they hung a banner that read, occupy space.

Walter—who now shared his home with Tiara, Bathsheba, Paul, Paul's wife (Lynne had joined him one day out of the blue, and they seemed to be repairing their marriage, or at least sharing the same bed), and Miss Adele and Miss Fisher's stockpile—would sometimes stand out on his back porch come evening, sipping on some vodka over ice and stare out over the tent city that stretched from treeline to treeline.

"Goddamn," he would say to himself, swaying gently in the humid night air. "Who'd've thought I'd have a Woodstock full of space hippies in my backyard one day?"

When the camp got big enough, fights and thefts and all kinds of just plain meanness set in, although not as much as one would expect, mostly because work left people too tired to fight, fuck, or commit felonies. But gather enough rocket heads in one place and you start to get a certain class of problem.

All day and all night, the camp sounded like a poorly organized fireworks display. At night, a thousand chemical campfires bloomed in vivid colors: bright red, emerald green, liquid-oxygen blue. During the day, a scrim of smoke from black-powder concussion caps hung over the tents like a bad mood.

Walter tried to bully his family "Support Crew" into policing the pyromaniacs, but they were overwhelmed just keeping the camp running. He tried to form another squad of enforcers, but you can't make rocket junkies police other rocket junkies, because if the combustible is really cool, they're going to want to play too. Then, in early July, a phalanx of eighteen Veterans for Peace, wearing desert fatigues and the odd prosthetic limb but reeking of sweat and pure badassery, marched up to Memomma's job table.

"I love men in uniform," she giggled, ignoring the fact that three of them were women.

They became the Goon Squad and they made it their life's mission to bring law and order to the camp. It took two days for people to learn that arguing with an ex-Marine who was permanently pissed off because a bunch of Iraqi insurgents had blown off his left hand was a losing proposition. A dispute-resolution center was set up, like a miniature court system, and pretty soon, the sundown hearings became the day's biggest entertainment.

But there was one problem that the Goon Squad couldn't stop: Randy Bates. They were able to shut down most of the more dangerous and careless chemical criminals, and sanctioned nighttime pyrotechnic displays were organized to filter off all that creative/psychotic/destructive energy, but Randy Bates was another class of problem.

Massively bearded and opposed to shoes for philosophical reasons, he was a welder gone bad. There was a court order to keep him from working with children after a horrifying incident with homemade fireworks and the Lake City Presbyterian Church Youth Group. His wife had left him after he'd blown off one of her fingers with a romantic, homemade palm-shell display in their backyard. When he heard that Walter Reddie was building a rocket, he'd sent his bank some jingle mail, loaded up his truck with anything that would bang, flash, or burn, and come to camp.

Since his arrival, he'd burned down three tents by accident and almost set the Mission Control barn on fire. He'd become an obsession for the Goon Squad, and they stalked him like the FBI. Somehow, even on a property this small, he kept one step ahead of them, sleeping in different tents every night, setting off home-made black-powder snappers every day, even shaving off his beard and putting on Tevas when they decided to watch the Port-a-Potties to catch him when he went to the john. He was warned, told off, had his powders and propellants confiscated, and sat down for a heart-to-heart with Walter over a big jelly glass of vodka, but it was all to no avail. Twenty minutes after every intervention, the steady *bang-bang-bang* would break out again all over the place. Finally, they had no choice but to admit failure and call the cops.

"You want this fellow off your land?" Sheriff Bennet Moore asked.

"Do what you got to do, Bennet," Walter said.

So, Bennet and two of his deputies walked into the campsite where Randy was sitting and they had a brief discussion. When it became clear that Randy wasn't going to move of his own accord, Bennet sighed deeply and signaled to the smaller of his two deputies, who tased Randy. Then the two deputies picked up the limp engineer and dragged him back to their squad car, his heels ploughing twin furrows in the dirt.

"You need to get in the car, too, Walt," Bennet said, hitching up his belt.

"Don't think I do, Bennet," Walter said. The Goon Squad rustled ominously.

"Call off your boys," Bennet said. "I've never tased a man with one leg before, but I'm always open to new experiences."

"They're not my boys to call off," Walter said. "They're free Americans who don't like the way this conversation is going."

"Man up and get in the car, Walt," Bennet said. "Huggies wants to speak to you."

Huggies was the not-so-affectionate nickname that everyone in Melville had for Mayor Hylance Huggins. He was the type of public employee who gave the impression of caring deeply about the problems of others while never actually doing anything about them. When asked, he would put his head next to yours and cry your tears for you, bemoaning the state of this fallen world that seemed to be particularly hard on you, then somehow, he'd leave without having done anything.

"I hear you, darling," he would say. "But if you want that toxic landfill shut down, we're going to have to raise the property taxes on everybody 'round here to pay for it. It'd make you mighty unpopular with your neighbors, you know."

"I feel you," he would moan at town meetings. "But to put up a traffic light would mean we've got to raise property taxes on everyone in town to pay for a traffic-pattern study, and an environmental impact assessment, and the installation of the system, and maintenance. Y'all'd be looking at big tax hikes for the next long while."

Despite all his poor-mouthing, Huggies somehow owned the laundromat, a barbeque restaurant, the biggest house in town, and one of only three pools in the county, and he seemed to be driving a new car every two years.

"All right, Bennet," Walter said. "I'll come see what Huggies wants, but put me in a different car than that jerk-off. The man hasn't showered in a week and he smells riper than roadkill."

So, Walt rode in high style in the front seat of Bennet's cruiser all the way to city hall, a small brick building that had once been a dentist's office before all the dentists had moved away because no one could afford to get their teeth cleaned anymore. Huggies was waiting in his office with Mr. Gaudy from the school.

"What say you, Walter? Have a seat! You want a Coke? Water? Coffee?" Huggies bubbled.

"I'll take a Coke," Walter said.

"What kind? We got Sprite, 7 UP, Mello Yello, Diet Coke."

"Diet Coke."

"I notice you're eyeballing Eugene there," Huggies said, indicating Mr. Gaudy. "He's come in as something of a special consultant this summer because of all the to-do."

"Special consultant on what?" Walter asked. "Ugly ties?"

"You're a joker, Walt," Huggies grinned. "But no, seriously, when I heard about what you were up to out at your place, I had two thoughts, three thoughts, really. You want to know what they were?"

"Not really."

"First, I was happy that you had found yourself a passion. We all need a passion, Walter. Keeps the mind sharp and the hands nimble. Second, I worried because I noticed you're attracting a bunch of unsavory types to your property. Third, I was concerned about the potential legal and liability issues this raised. So, I called in Eugene here, as he's a man of science on his summer vacation, and I asked him to review the issues."

"I'll agree with you about one thing," Walt said. "He is an expert on unsavory characters."

"You know that is not the Mayor's meaning," Mr. Gaudy snipped.

"The unsavory types, we'll deal with them later," Huggies said. "But I wanted you to hear what he has to say so you can have a chance to clean this up yourself before the full force of the law has to do it for you. Eugene, tell Walt what you said yesterday."

"I want to hear it from his lips first," Mr. Gaudy said. "Are you building a spaceship, Walter?"

"It's called a spacecraft," Walter said. "And it's just a little bitty thing. What we're focusing most of our energy on is the launch vehicle. That's the one that's going to involve half a million tons of high explosives."

"Christ on a crutch." Huggies whistled.

"You realize that you have no chance of success," Mr. Gaudy said.

"Probably not," Walter agreed.

"Just the legal issues alone are overwhelming," Mr. Gaudy said. He pulled a stack of papers out of a fussy little plastic folder. "I've familiarized myself with a few of them. First, you'll have to have an FAA waiver to route air traffic out of the flight area before you can purchase any kind of fuel or even parts for a rocket. You'll need a low explosives permit for your fuel from the Bureau of Alcohol, Tobacco, Firearms and Explosives, which will require building ATF-compliant structures for storage and safe handling. The Office of Commercial Space Transportation will need to grant you separate licenses for both take-off and reentry. Have you applied for one of those yet?"

"Not personally," Walter admitted.

"You'll have to undergo a pre-application consultation, a policy review, a safety review, a payload review, and determination hearing, a financial-responsibility determination, and an environmental review. Are you prepared to undertake any of these processes?"

"Not as such."

"This will have to be cleared with the State Department, the Department of Defense, NASA, the FCC, the Department of Commerce, NOAA, all relevant US trade representatives, and if your flight path passes over Canada or Mexico or even Jamaica, you will have to have written declarations from those governments granting their permission."

"If you say so."

"Launching your rocket will also violate several arms-control treaties which regulate all rocket and missile launches. You are about to commit treason, you are about to violate the sovereign airspace of at least one other nation, and you just sit there, smelling of strong spirits, and shrug."

"I sort of just planned on skipping all this paperwork," Walter said.

"Do you even have insurance?"

"Never been a big fan of betting against myself," Walter said.

"You have to have insurance. The Space Shuttle is indemnified by the federal government for one point five billion dollars in third party damages, but they won't indemnify you. And you're going to have to carry a large liability policy to receive any clearances."

"People say the same thing about car insurance, but I just pay the ticket. It's cheaper."

"Okay, Walter," Huggies said. "I know this all sounds

like a big joke to you, but it's a serious matter. Imagine what would happen if there was an accident out at your place. People could get hurt. Or what if you get that rocket into the sky and it crashes right on down through city hall? Or what if it hits my house? I just built an outdoor pizza oven out back, and it cost me a pretty chunk of change. I don't want it to get turned into a smoking crater by your rocket."

"You've got no call to shut me down," Walter said. "I haven't violated any laws."

"You're about to."

"You want to start making arrests, you send Bennet on up to my place," Walter said. "There's close to three hundred people up there. We'll see how good he and his sixteen deputies do with them."

"Don't make me call the governor," Huggies said.

"He wouldn't take your call," Walter said.

"Think about what you're doing," Mr. Gaudy said. "You're endangering the lives of thousands of people with your redneck NASA."

"Everyone is up there of their own free will," Walter said. "And as for the people around here, well, I'm very sorry that my rocket might crash through their roofs and put a premature halt to their careers as professional television watchers, but given the state of the economy, I might actually be doing them a favor."

"You're completely insane," Mr. Gaudy said.

"Nope," Walter said. "From where I'm sitting, you're

the insane one. A license to go into orbit? Fuck that noise. You can't make me get a license to exercise my God-given right as an American to go into space and rescue my cousin. Me and my 'redneck NASA' are the only ones who give a shit about that boy."

"Your arrogance is breathtaking," Mr. Gaudy said.

"Probably is. Now, look here, Huggies, either send Bennet up there to arrest everyone or have him give me a ride back."

In the end, Mayor Huggins blinked, but it wasn't a total victory. Walter had to walk back to his farm. It took him the better part of three hours.

Walter told the story when he got back, and it tore through camp like a stomach flu. From then on, they had a name: Redneck NASA. Two days later, it appeared on a giant sign hung over the gate to Walt's property.

Nothing could stand in Redneck NASA's way. No problem could resist three hundred brains and unlimited muscle for very long. When exotic problems started to crop up, Memomma would just open up her Excel spreadsheet, and within an hour they'd locate an expert somewhere in the camp. The few fields that were so specialized that the number of experts in the world could be counted on one hand were only a Zoom call or a Facebook message away. By now, word had spread, and most people in the field were willing to trade a bit of their knowledge to talk to the madmen at Redneck NASA.

A second and then a third prefabricated building went up by the barn, and that's where the three rockets that made up the launch vehicle started to come together. Everyone had been working based on purest optimism, but it wasn't until the first load of steel plate arrived that people realized that this might actually happen. When the first truck delivering steel began nosing its way through the camp, Redneck NASA got galvanized.

The team fabricating the launch vehicle put the sheet metal on a brake and began bending it into enormous cylinders. They would be crammed with fuel to provide the twenty-four thousand, eight hundred and eighty-four mph speed that the spacecraft needed to achieve escape velocity. The spacecraft itself was being built on the other side of the back pasture, under a large Army Surplus field hospital tent that someone had bought for a few hundred dollars and patched to within an inch of its life.

There was no doubt that Walter was going to be the astronaut going up. Part of the reason was that he was the only one with the experience, even though he was draining the budget to keep himself in Popov. The vodka was a worry, and Tiara tried to discuss it with Paul, who found the subject uncomfortable and weaseled out of it every time it came up. Besides, Walt's most important qualification wasn't that he was sober; it was that he was completely suicidal. He honestly did not care whether he lived or died, and even though hybrid rockets were safer than liquid- or solid-propellant rockets, it still required someone with zero consideration for their own personal safety to agree to strap themselves to the end of one of them.

The camp kept growing. Come July, there were five hundred people living there full-time, and on weekends the part-timers and hobbyists flooded in and pushed that number closer to eight hundred. Then eleven hundred. Then fifteen hundred. The camp went tribal. Teams for Launch Vehicle Design & Manufacture were formed, then a Launch Operations Team came together; Miss Adele and Miss Fisher headed Procurement, while Flight Management was run by Paul and Tiara. Paul attracted the other unemployed rocket nerds, while Tiara attracted a large flock of smitten boys and young women with belly-button piercings who followed her around and hung on her every calculation.

Making her even more of an asset was the fact that she was Black. Seeing a sister on the project gave it a stamp of approval in parts of the county where Walt had never been. Boys he would have thought should be arrested, wearing braids and with their pants hanging off their behinds, started showing up and working the wiring. A six-foot-four, soft-spoken linebacker whose attendance record meant he barely graduated tenth grade turned out to speak fluent ballistics. A trio of Rastafarian metalworkers materialized, and the welds on the fuel tanks became things of beauty. Tiara had access to a world of talent no one had much thought to tap before.

July slipped away and August began, humid as hell, and with it came Bobby Junior's birthday. Walt knew that Gail would be talking to him in the morning (Jimmy Royal gave her a discount price on the call because he was such a Christian), but Walt wanted to speak to Bobby in the evening slot when no one else was around.

A couple of weeks before, Bobby had been briefly back in the news when Richard Branson had announced that his prototype Space Plane had made it into space for a few seconds, and now he was building his Virgin Space Plane Mark II, and any minute he'd be heading up to rescue the boy. A few days later, Bobby Junior had faded from the news again. Everyone wanted to forget the fact that he was circling over their heads at hundreds of miles per hour, waiting to die, and they'd all put him there. The government certainly didn't want to call attention to it, and with a midterm election coming up and a rash of school shootings all over the country, there were plenty of other things for the media to cover.

That night, Walt drove his truck to Jimmy Royal's place and handed him a check for fifty dollars, then waited for Jimmy to arrange the satellite uplink. The first thing he did was send a packet of digital images. Then he waited for the second pass.

"Bobby, this is Melville. Over."

Silence.

"Bobby, this is Melville. Over."

"I read you, Melville. This is Bobby Campbell Junior on the ISS. Over."

"You get the pictures? Over."

"Received. Over."

"What do you think?"

The silence went on so long, Walt thought they'd lost contact. Then:

"You all're really building this thing? Over."

"I'm afraid we are. Over."

"That's a real rocket you're building down there. Over."

"That's what I been trying to tell you all along, you little asswipe. Over."

"You're really coming to save me? Over."

"We're going to try. Over."

"Thank you. Thank all y'all. I knew my people wouldn't forget me."

"Don't start crying like a big girl just yet; I got a birthday present for you. I want you to give her a name. Over."

Silence for a minute, and then it came through loud and true.

"Name her *Space Jesus* for me, Walter. Because she's gonna save me from damnation. Over."

"Copy that, Bobby. Hang in there, big man. Help is coming. Over."

But by then, Bobby Junior had fallen out of the window, and the ISS continued its crazed orbit around a planet that no longer cared. Only *Space Jesus* could save him now.

TWO

It was the vodka that killed all those horses. More specifically, it was the vodka circulating in Walter Reddie's bloodstream that made him decide to handle the welding of the test stand himself when they were getting ready to test the gas vanes. These were the vanes that protruded into the hot gas jet at the rear of the engine, and they would turn to steer the rocket, giving it vector thrust control. It was the vodka in Walter's veins that made him belligerently take over the welding from the Rastas because he "wanted some shit to do," and that made him decide the job was finished without double-checking the integrity of his weld.

The next day, the prototype engine was chained to the test stand, and the immediate area was cleared. The countdown began over the loudspeaker and then the engine was remote-fired. It was built to generate seven miles per second of thrust, enough for escape velocity, which meant that, basically, they were strapping down an incredibly powerful missile. The second it fired, the welds failed, and the engine tore itself free of the chains at the base of the mount and shot into the air, flying in an arcing, upward trajectory like a football kicked towards a field goal.

People watched it fly with a mixture of terror and

pride: pride because their engine was far more powerful than they had imagined. No one had thought that they were building something that could attain this kind of altitude. On paper, sure. But in real life, they had all doubted it a little bit. Terror because they all knew it had to come down somewhere.

Somewhere turned out to be the horse barn at Territory Hill, a bit of private property six miles from Walter Reddie's farm where some investment bankers had stashed their high-end polo ponies imported from Argentina. Most of them didn't play much these days, but they hired ringers to ride their horses for teams of rich Brits playing polo in the Virgin Islands.

The jet engine came hurtling out of the sky like a pony-hating comet, smashing into one end of the stable and releasing all its kinetic energy in a shock wave that killed six of the eight horses instantaneously. The remaining two were pumped so full of shrapnel, they had to be put down. Walter was drunk, but he wasn't drunk enough not to know what to expect next.

By the time Bennet and his boys showed up, Walter was waiting for them all alone out by the highway, away from the Goon Squad. He put his hands behind his back and let them put him under arrest, flexi-cuff him, and load him into the squad car. Bennet started reciting the charges but got bored after the fifth or sixth one and asked if it was okay to stop. Walter nodded, his vodka-filled head sloshing loosely on the end of his neck.

He sat in a cell for half the day and only saw someone when one of the deputies—he thought it was the Pruitt boy—brought him a tray for lunch. His stomach had gone sour and his head was throbbing, so he didn't much feel like eating. He passed out for a while at that point, waking up once to vomit weakly, then he lay back down and fell into a depressed sleep.

The next morning, they woke him up and gave him some oatmeal. He barely managed to keep it down. His body felt like it was stuffed full of broken lightbulbs, and all his previous confidence felt hollow and false. One of the deputies told him that a crowd of Rocket Zombies had gathered overnight outside the tiny police station, filling the parking lot and spilling out into the street. They were mostly peaceful and quiet, but as the morning wore on, more and more of them appeared until they surrounded the police station a couple of hundred deep. It was an intimidating sight, and it made Bennet load up his men with pepper spray.

"Just in case antifa tries to stir up some shit," he said.

The crowd was ominously quiet, which freaked the police out even more. Inside the station, it felt like they were under siege, and really, even Bennet knew there wasn't much they could do against the crowd if they decided to rush the doors. After all, pepper spray wasn't much more than high-pressure Texas Pete. It wouldn't stop a hundred people, let alone a thousand.

Towards noon, two deputies came to his holding cell and took Walter down the hall to the sole interview room, and sat him opposite Huggies.

"Given the crap-load of rioters out there, I thought it was best if I came to you," Huggies said. "So, Walter, why'd you kill your wife?"

"What?" Walter asked. His poor aching head was still throbbing.

"Kidding, kidding," Huggies said. "I've always wanted to say that. Too many *Law & Order* episodes. Now, how do I make those people go away?"

"I'm not their boss," Walter said. "They come and go as they please."

"So, if you went out there and ordered that they immediately disperse…"

"It'd mean fuck-all," Walter said. "You got any aspirin?"

"Hey, Bennet!" Huggies hollered, knocking on the two-way mirror. "Get some aspirin for this drunkard, would you?"

"Who else is back there?" Walter asked.

"Just Eugene. I don't want a big audience for this."

"Is this the part where you lock me up and throw away the key?"

"You know how many people you got living up on that farm?"

"A bunch?"

"Bennet says his girl deputy counted close to one

thousand, eight hundred. They started camping on Claude's land next door."

"I never told them to trespass."

"Well, Claude's been foreclosed for a long time, and to be honest with you, I don't think the bank's going to make a whole lot of noise over it. But boy, Walter, almost two thousand people? And Bennet's girl says more are coming. How many you think you'll have by the end of summer? Three thousand? Four?"

"They're not my responsibility," Walter said.

"That's where you're wrong," Huggies said. "You told those people you were going to fly your rocket ship into space to rescue Bobby Junior, and that got their hopes up, and that got them here. Eugene says the lawyers call it incitement."

"I don't think Eugene Gaudy is who you should be getting legal advice from," Walter said.

"We're beyond legality now," Huggies said. "We're all the way over into morality at this point."

"Last time I checked, you didn't have no authority over morality."

"Did you know that Mrs. Huggins is on your parachute team? She is. Your Memomma rounded up all the folks who knew how to sew, and my better half has been going up to your place twice a week to sew since late July."

"It's a free country."

"My point is," Huggies said, "that if I hold you,

those people outside are going to cause a fracas, and I hate fracas. The fact that the entire town smells like an open sewer from Lord knows how many Port-a-Potties you got up at your place is a mess and a menace and it aggravates me.

"But I also have to admit, with all these people, the Waffle House is doing gangbuster business, and our Wal-Mart is number one in the region. Juan's Automotive tells me they've done over $18,000 in special orders for your people. On top of that, Mrs. Huggins has been more considerate towards her marital duties ever since she started doing something besides watching TV and fretting over Ethan. You know my boy? Got a communications degree. What the hell does that even mean?"

"What are you trying to tell me, Huggies?"

"What I'm trying to tell you is that we are in a state of delicate balance. The morality of the situation overrides the legality. I'm going to agree to let you proceed with this insanity, and the town of Melville will assist you where it can in violating numerous federal and state laws."

"Are you kidding me?"

"Listen, Walter," Huggies said, leaning over the table and lowering his voice. "Eugene's not the only one who can look up the law. I talked to a fellow over in Greenville, and he's drawn up a whole bunch of paperwork that completely and totally protects my ass in case this thing goes south. Don't tell Eugene, but I've made him deputy mayor acting in absentia. You know, on paper."

"He's your fall guy?"

"Keep it down. Eugene's not a bad guy; he just thinks being a tight-ass is in his job description."

"I knew you'd play the angles," Walter said, shaking his head in wonder. "This goes good: you're a hero. It goes bad: not your fault."

"Before it goes anywhere, I got a condition and I got a warning."

Walter waited for Huggies to ask him for a payout. He wondered if you could pay a bribe with Venmo or if it absolutely had to be cash.

"The condition is, you got to stop drinking. Judging by the way you seem to be suffering from a monstrous hangover this morning, I have to assume that those dead horses over at Territory Hill are on account of all that vodka you got floating around in your bloodstream. Am I right?"

"Maybe," Walter said, feeling truly ashamed for the first time in a long while.

"If you want this to proceed, you need to stop drinking. You say you're an astronaut? Act like one."

"I don't know if I can do that."

"I'm serious, Walter; you're going to have to undergo random urine screens."

"What the hell, Huggies?"

"If you want this town to help you potentially start a

nuclear war, then by God, you're going to be sober while you do it. Plus, the town's insurance company says that we need to do due diligence in order to avoid liability if you ever actually get this thing off the ground.

"Eugene has the dubious honor of collecting your urine and monitoring the results. And you know how he prides himself on busting your chops, so don't even think about trying to cheat. If I know Eugene, he's going to insist on standing next to you at the commode with you while you produce your sample."

Walter wasn't entirely sure he could open his mouth again without retching, so he was disinclined to argue. He nodded.

"I'm glad we reached this understanding," Huggies smiled. He rapped on the two-way mirror. "Bennet, bring this man some aspirin so he can go outside and disperse that unlawful gathering. And Eugene, bring in that paperwork."

It was a liability waiver. Walter signed it without even reading all the way through. As he got up to go, Huggies stopped him.

"As for that warning, Walt," he said, "you're going to walk outside to see a couple thousand people. You got close to two thousand up at your camp. They're all expecting to launch a rocket into space. Be very sure about what you're doing, because God help you if you don't deliver. Crowds got a way of turning into mobs real quick."

* * *

Later that night, Walter sat down privately and explained the new conditions to Tiara.

"That's good," she said. "I've been waiting for you to, um, sort of start astronaut training."

"There ain't a lot of training I can do," Walter said. "Look around, this is just a big camp full of hippies. Not a lot of specialized equipment here."

"What kind of equipment do you need?" Tiara asked. "Can't you go running or something? You look pretty bad."

Instinctively, Walter wanted to argue, but for once, he stopped himself. He knew she was right. Everyone was doing their job —more than their job, actually — and it was time for him to do his. Tomorrow. He'd have one last drinking session tonight, and then tomorrow he'd get started. He went in the kitchen to get a glass. Standing by the sink was a boy in a cape pouring out his gallon jug of Popov.

"What the hell're you doing!" Walter yelled, grabbing the nearest thing at hand, which happened to be a hammer, and running at the kid.

"Don't hit me!" the kid said, reflexively throwing up his hands and, in the process, tossing the half-full plastic jug of Popov against the wall. The room filled with the eye-watering stink of cheap vodka.

"What the fuck!?!?" Walter yelled.

"Lady Tiara sent me," the kid said. "She told me I would be your personal fitness monitor."

At that point, Walter noticed that the kid was wearing a leather shoe string tied around his forehead. He had peach fuzz that looked like a caterpillar was sleeping on his upper lip, and a braided ponytail.

"What the fuck is your name?"

"I LARP as the human blacksmith, Volor."

"I don't even know what that means."

"Men call me Volor."

"Fuck off."

"I can't," the kid said. He shifted from foot to foot. "The Lady Tiara would be really, really pissed if I left."

For the rest of the night, the kid followed Walter around and Walt had to admit he showed a talent for ferreting out his hidden stashes of booze. He even poured out all the Listerine.

"My mom was a big-time alcoholic before she found Jesus," the kid explained.

By the time he was ready for bed, Walter had gotten used to being tailed by this sunken-chested geek. He had a hard time falling asleep sober, so he asked the kid to tell him about his life, and before he had even reached the tenth boring minute, Walter was snoring gently.

He woke up at 4 AM like he'd been shot. Volor was standing at the end of his bed, yanking on his foot.

"Time to go running, Mr. Reddie," he said.

"Drop dead, Volor," Walter said.

Volor looked around nervously, then he began to sing in a piercing, reedy wail:

> *"Listen my muggle friend,*
> *To a tale that's often told*
> *Of a boy who lived beneath the stair…"*

"What the fuck is wrong with you?" Walt asked.

> *"And an evil cursed and old.*
> *Of a school for magic true*
> *And a heart both stout and pure…"*

The singing sounded like something you'd hear at a funeral, and it made Walt's eardrums vibrate painfully. He dragged himself out of bed and hid from the kid in the bathroom for a while, hawking up some yellow crud. Then he pulled on some clothes he hadn't worn since 1995, and he went running. He didn't want to risk that hideous singing again.

The air was moist and dark. Cicadas screamed in the trees. From the fabrication assembly shed, he could see the flickering of welding. Volor followed him a respectful twenty yards behind. Silently.

He'd been coasting. He knew it. And now he was embarrassed to find out that other people knew it, too. He wanted to impress Volor with the fact that when push came to shove, he still had what it took, but after a hundred yards his knees felt like they'd been pounded with rocks and his ankles felt like skin stretched around broken glass. After two hundred yards, he was breathing so hard, his chest hurt.

His feet slapped the road and, slow as a beetle, he trundled on, doing about two miles before coming home. He only threw up once. Those other three times were just the dry heaves. Volor easily kept pace with him, even though he was still wearing his velvet cloak. As the sun came up, Volor brought him to the medical tent and asked one of the nurses to give Walt a full physical. The results weren't encouraging, but they weren't a disaster, either. By the time noon rolled around, Walter was on a new diet and he had a health plan in place. Volor would hold him to it.

Around two PM, as Walter was leaving the medical tent, a runner brought some ugly but not entirely unexpected news.

"Mr. Reddie," the kid shouted. Walter really wished that if these kids were going to stick steel bars through their nipples, they'd at least wear shirts so he didn't have to look at their brutalized boy nips. "The principal's here and he's got some fascist police state thugs with him."

Walter met up with them at the gate where the Goon Squad was refusing to let them pass. It turned out that the Big Government Thugs were three pencil-necked officials from the FAA and one all-business lady from the AST (Office of Commercial Space Transportation—the acronym had never made sense to Walter, either).

"Afternoon, fellas," Walter said, extending his hand. "Walter Reddie, *Discovery*, crew of '86. Pleased to meet you. And this is Volor, my personal trainer."

"Greetings," Volor said, sweeping his cape and bowing low.

"I'm Dr. Huger," the AST woman, said. "We need a quiet place to sit down and talk."

"We can talk right here," Walter said. "Unless you've got something embarrassing to say that you want privacy for."

"See," Mr. Gaudy said. "I told you. He has no respect for anyone or anything."

"Eugene," Walter said. "You've got it all mixed up. I have plenty of respect for lots of people and lots of things; I just don't have any for you."

"Boys," Dr. Huger said. "I understand that this is some kind of ritualistic macho behavior, but there are serious matters to discuss, and if Mr. Reddie won't discuss them in private, we'll discuss them in public."

"Sounds fair to me," Walter said. "You're the first person who's made a lick of sense all afternoon. Why don't me and Volor show you around first?"

And so they took a tour. It turned out to be a huge mistake. He led them to the original barn, now known as Mission Control, and introduced them to Paul and Tiara and Paul's Big Brains. Paul actually knew Dr. Huger from the AST and had to be convinced to come out from his hiding place behind a rack of servers to shake hands with her. She held on to his hand for an extra minute.

"Paul," she said. "I never thought I'd see you involved in something like this."

"I..." Paul said. "I just... Well, you see..."

"There's nothing really that dangerous about it," Tiara piped up. "It's no more dangerous than driving a car or, um, flying a plane."

"Unless you're a horse," Dr. Huger said. "I heard that you people were refusing to pay the owners' claims."

"There's no way a goddamn horse costs that much money!" Walter said.

As far as he was concerned, these rich pricks saw an opportunity to get a payday.

"We don't regulate spaceflight because we want to rain on your parade," Dr. Huger said. "We do it because you have no idea how much trouble it could cause if everyone started building launch sites all over America. We are signatories to several international treaties. What happens if you launch? What happens when a Chinese or North Korean satellite shows a rocket, unannounced, lifting off from American soil? They might think it's a nuclear missile. It could conceivably be taken as an act of aggression."

"No, it won't," Tiara said. "They're not dumb."

"No, but they might be looking for an excuse to act out. Raise some questions in the UN, get sanctions leveled against the United States. That kind of thing."

After that, the tour only got worse. The camp really did smell like an outhouse since the wind was blowing north that morning, and seeing it all through these strangers' eyes made the place look even more ramshackle and tawdry than it normally did to Walter.

He saw the rocket shop, and instead of being impressed by how far along the launch vehicle was, it looked to him like some kind of big, shoddy toy slapped together by morons. Who was he kidding to think this thing could go up into space?

No one was impressed by the machine shop, either. Or the tool-repair shack, or the metal works. No one looked at the rebuilt launchpad and saw the hundreds of man-hours that had been poured into it. Instead, they saw its uneven surface and crumbling edges. When they saw the six-hundred-thousand-gallon liquid-fuel tank that had a new cryogenic refrigeration system installed and ready to be tested that afternoon, they didn't see a miracle of mechanical engineering, built from scratch by a bunch of people who didn't have anything to lose. They saw a ticking time bomb waiting to explode.

They didn't want to say anything while they were surrounded by all the Big Brains and Rocket Zombies, but two hours later when the little tour finally wound its way back to the gate, they let Walter know that they were taking a dim view of Redneck NASA, and they spelled out in no uncertain terms what had to happen next.

"You'll have to shut it down," Dr. Huger said. "We'll give you three days to shut it down yourself and send all these people home, or else we'll come in here and shut it down for you."

"I can understand that from your point of view..." Walter began.

"This is not a question of perspective," Dr. Huger said. "This is a question of an imminent danger. You clearly have some kind of a death wish and I can't address that, but I can address the fact that you have no regard for the safety of the people in your charge. You have led these children down the garden path, and it's time to send them home before more than horses get hurt."

"These aren't children. They can decide what risks they're willing to take for themselves."

"We're not a bunch of paper-pushing bureaucrats, Mr. Reddie," Dr. Huger said. "We have regulations and laws for a reason. It's called living in a society. We all choose to obey them so that this country can function."

"Your regs are a joke," Walter said.

"A joke?" Dr. Huger turned pale and tight-lipped. "We aren't asking you to do these things for your health. These regulations are here to keep these people from dying. We won't allow launches on days without five miles of visibility because it's too dangerous. What if you hit a commercial aircraft? Or a satellite because you don't have real-time tracking? You can't launch within five thousand feet of a building, because you will set it on fire. These aren't rules made by a bunch of nervous Nellies to ruin your little rocket party. They are made because what you are trying to do here will kill people who have not been informed of the risks."

"I think we're a little beyond how close to the buildings we are," Walter said. "We're way beyond that now. This thing, I couldn't shut it down if I wanted to. And I don't want to, anyways."

Lookouts on the road suddenly started blowing whistles and yelling "Five Oh! Five Oh!" Walter sighed. Today just kept getting better and better. He watched as Sheriff Bennet pulled into his driveway, leading two other squad cars up the dirt road. It was the entire Melville PD. Mr. Gaudy grinned as Bennet and his deputies got out, hitched up their belts, and hung their nightsticks on them.

"I thought we had a deal," Walter said as the fat man strode over.

"No deal that I'm aware of," Bennet said. "I'm just coming up here to do my duty as a peace officer."

"It's about time," Mr. Gaudy said.

"Walt, are these folks bothering you?" Bennet asked.

"These folks?"

"Yep, these Federal types. They up here on your property at your invitation?"

"Not particularly."

"You want them to leave?"

"I get the picture," Dr. Huger said. "Up with people.

Solidarity. You're all on the same side. We're going. But know this: people are going to get hurt here. Some of them may even die. And I'm not going to let that happen."

"Unless you know something I don't, everyone up here's going to die eventually," Walt said. "These people just finally found something worth dying for."

"You want to sacrifice them to your selfish craving to go back up in space," Dr. Huger said. "These folks may not recognize it, but I've been around astronauts all my life, Mr. Reddie. I can recognize Old Astronaut Syndrome when I see it."

"All right, ma'am," Bennet said. "I just need you to step this way. I think Walt's tired of your visit now."

"I don't have to tell you that this isn't going to end well, do I?" Dr. Huger asked.

"The only way this is going to end," Walt said, "is with our rocket in space."

"No," she said. "The way it's going to end is with you in handcuffs."

As Bennet's deputies ushered the FAA and AST officials away, Mr. Gaudy stood his ground.

"What do you want, Eugene?" Walt asked, tired of all this nonsense. It was barely one o'clock and his body ached.

"I want your urine," Mr. Gaudy said, pulling a plastic sample cup out of his briefcase. "In this receptacle."

"Man, I just stopped drinking yesterday. There's been no time to flush anything out of my system."

"All the more reason to do the first screen right this minute. We can establish a baseline."

"You're going to want to watch, aren't you?"

"Don't think your discomfort won't give me a great degree of satisfaction," Mr. Gaudy said.

"Come on, Volor," Walt said, starting the trudge back to the house. "You might as well watch too."

After that, Walter could smell the end coming. Local news segments gave way to national news coverage, and Melville motels filled up as the press poured into town and barfed big piles of money onto the shoes of anyone with a spare room. Huggies had marked up the prices on his rental properties to ruinous levels, and CNN, MSNBC, and Fox were shoving bricks of cash at him. Tea Party loyalists like the Beauforts had so many correspondents from Taiwanese news channels and Al Jazeera staying together in their converted garage apartment that even Oddie Beaufort was eating hummus now.

The Chinese press, in particular, loved the fact that the most vital sector of the American space program was located on a thirty-acre farm in South Carolina, a state whose former claims to fame were televangelists, being broke, and starting the Civil War. Xinhua issued nightly updates on Redneck NASA, and China's snarky coverage was becoming an embarrassment to NASA, to the FAA, and to the government of the United States of America. There was no way this could be allowed to continue.

And so they picked up the pace. Jimmy was on the ham with Bobby Junior almost every time the window opened, getting trajectory updates as the station's orbit decayed. More Rocket Zombies showed up every day, and both the launch team and the manufacturing team were burning through all this new human capital like coal thrown in a furnace. The camp was a train, humans were its fuel, and it was going too fast to stop. People worked until they collapsed, slept where they fell, then woke up and got right back to work.

On September 1, Paul announced that *Space Jesus* was ready to emerge from manufacturing and move to the launch platform, and that night, there was much rejoicing. When the sun cut through the trees the next morning, eight hundred Rocket Zombies were standing outside an enormous ragged hole ripped in the metal skin of the rocket assembly barn. The night before, Uncle AJ had noticed that the rockets were too big to fit through the doors, so he'd armed a work crew with hatchets and peeled the entire side of the barn open as neatly as you'd crack a can of beans.

The three rockets were just metal skins pulled over propulsion systems, and once on the launch platform and welded to each other, the massive pressure chambers at the top of each of them would be stuffed with one hundred and sixty-six thousand, six hundred and sixty-six pounds of liquid oxygen each. The liquid oxygen would be put under insane pressure, then over a quarter million pounds of black polyurethane rods would be slotted into the bottom two-thirds of rocket. This was the solid fuel that would provide the thrust. Once loaded, they would be impossible to move, but even empty, each of the three rockets that made up *Space Jesus* (blasphemously named the Father, the Son, and the Holy Ghost) weighed closed to one hundred thousand pounds.

Paul had a crew up all night making rollers out of wood, scrap steel, anything they could get their hands on, and these were placed underneath each of the massive rockets which were laid horizontal, then they began to move them. They moved them the way the Israelites built the pyramids: almost one thousand Rocket Zombies pressed close, pushing hard, using nothing more than human muscle. The Father went first, and as it left rollers behind, Rocket Zombies raced them to the front just in time to catch the Father's nose, like moving a Viking ship from dry dock to the sea.

News crews were tripping over each other's cables as they walked backwards, filming the most primitive rocket rollout in the history of man. It was one part NASA, two parts caveman. There was something intoxicating about this exercise in brute force, and the few people not in the horde began to clap and cheer and the cheers turned to chants and the clapping became rhythmic and it took on the qualities of a pagan ritual. When one of the Rocket Zombies stumbled and went to her knees, a sound engineer for MSNBC was so caught up in the moment that he grabbed her roller and took her place in the shuffling horde.

It was slow, sweaty work. The rollers groaned. Three of the wooden ones shattered. The concrete approach ramp cracked under their weight. The longer the day wore on, the more the happy shouts and songs of the kids seemed like taunts. The sun hammered down on the Rocket Zombies, mosquitoes swarmed around their faces. Good spirits curdled and died. But finally, eventually, after it slid off the concrete path twice, after the concrete shattered and had to be patched once, after two people twisted their ankles, and after fifteen people were pulled from the crew for torn shoulders and broken fingers, the Father was in position.

Winches screamed, and scaffolding cracked like gunshots as it took the weight of the Father. Then, at a horrifyingly slow pace, its nose left the ground, then its midsection, and Rocket Zombies swarmed, using the rollers as poles now to push up on the Father, keeping all its weight from transferring to where its base rested on the ground. It was like watching an Egyptian obelisk being raised for the first time, and finally it was done.

The Father towered over them, painted pink by the setting sun.

As if they had suddenly been slain, eight hundred Rocket Zombies flopped over backwards and groans rose from their mouths. The kitchen crew sent runners with mugs of stew, and as the first crew hauled their shattered bodies from the launch platform, the ready team of another thousand Rocket Zombies took their places and prepared to move the Son.

When the third and final crew keeled over in their tracks they fell onto grass wet with morning dew. It had taken them twenty-four hours to move the three rockets. As the third team of broken and shattered Rocket Zombies dragged themselves away from the launchpad after getting the Holy Ghost in place at dawn, the next team swarmed and, with the speed and efficiency of angry ants, they erected curtains of scaffolding all around the hundred-foot-tall launch vehicles. The Father, the Son, and the Holy Ghost were yoked together and welded into place.

When the welding was finished around six PM, after all the news crews had filed their stories and gone to bed, the tiny spacecraft was rolled out of its construction tent. Compared to the rockets, it was a baby. It only took twenty-eight people to carry it. They hooked it on to chains and winched it up into the sky. The pilot, Walter, would be launched standing, strapped in with a four-point safety belt recycled from a NASCAR vehicle. Below his feet was a padded shelf with another four-point belt, where Bobby Jr would be strapped in for the return trip. Walter would fly fully suited and with his helmet on so that they didn't have to fully pressurize the compartment.

Building a spacesuit was beyond their capabilities because it required too much structural engineering and too many exotic materials. Anyways, an actual spacesuit would be too big for the tiny, tubular spacecraft, so they'd bought an old, experimental Russian CAC suit. It used mechanical counterpressure instead of air pressure to maintain biological integrity in low-pressure environments. It was skintight with a massive helmet at one end that looked like an inverted fish bowl out of a 1950s sci-fi movie.

"I don't want to be shoved into some kind of Commie trash bag," Walter had complained.

"There aren't any alternatives," Paul had answered. "It's the 'Commie trash bag' or you don't fly."

"You can't tell me what to do," Walt said.

"I'm simply stating a fact. This has become bigger than you now. I have got a host of people to choose from, all of them eager to put on the CAC suit and go up into space."

"None with my experience," Walt said.

"None with your health problems, either."

Walter agreed to wear it. Reluctantly.

It took them two days and nights of burning to

coordinate and integrate all the various systems on the launchpad between Mission Control, *Space Jesus*, and the Father, the Son, and the Holy Ghost. Then came the delivery. That's when things got serious.

Buying half a million pounds of highly combustible liquid oxygen tends to attract the attention of international law enforcement, and in this case, as the first tractor-trailer lumbered up the road to Walt's farm, it was being tracked by the FBI. The local office had expected an al-Qaeda terrorist cell at first, then changed their expectations to a domestic terrorist group, and now, after several phone calls from Dr. Huger at the AST, they had no idea what they were looking at. Space Nazis? Moon terrorists? Low Earth orbit militia? Whatever it was, it definitely wasn't legal.

Paul's crew backed the nine-thousand-gallon reefer truck up to the giant cryogenic fuel tank behind Mission Control, just the way they'd rehearsed all week. Once it had been laboriously backed into place, they chocked the wheels and drew a one-gallon sample of the bright blue liquid oxygen. Paul signed for the load and then he sent everyone except Tiara far away. It probably wasn't far enough to protect them from a real accident, but it might be okay if they had a minor mishap.

They dragged the braided steel hose over to the truck

and locked the coupling around the discharge valve. Paul got the signal that the team on the other side of the enormous fuel tank was ready to vent air as the liquid oxygen entered the freezing cold chamber.

"We don't need a license to be doing this or anything, do we?" Tiara asked.

Paul opened the discharge valve and felt the metal hose begin sucking liquid oxygen into the storage tank.

"Tiara," he said. "Imagine cooling air to minus one hundred and eighty-three degrees Celsius. A temperature so low that its atomic structure collapses into a liquid state. So low that it becomes eight hundred and sixty times more concentrated than regular oxygen. Oxygen causes rust, it causes fire, it's one of the great corrosive and combustible gases on this planet, so imagine it concentrated eight hundred and sixty times. If you spill it, it will instantly evaporate and create a super-oxygenized zone that will burst into flame at the slightest spark. Do you think that substance, the one we are pumping right now, requires a license to move several hundred thousand tons of it? A substance that dangerous? Think about it."

Tiara thought about it, and the more she thought about, it the more nervous she got about the liquid oxygen rushing past her knees at thirteen hundred gallons per minute. Cold sweat prickled across her forehead, her palms got slick, she felt something trickle down the small of her back. Then the sound of the pump rose three octaves and they shut it down and uncoupled the hose. Tiara let her spine unstiffen. Paul slapped her on the back.

"Look alive," he said. "We've got eight more truck-loads to get through today."

THREE

If you're the FBI Special Agent in Charge who is conducting surveillance on a bunch of what appear to be a lot of extremists building a giant missile, with an eye towards making eventual arrests, then you have access to a lot of resources. In fact, you have access to so many resources that they all start breathing down your neck. SAC John Richter was feeling the pressure.

The domestic terrorists had originally been reported to him by the resident agency in Spartanburg, and SAC Richter had immediately followed protocol and initiated observation. He'd sent word of new developments up the chain of command, and the word from on high was to wait until the targets had acquired materials of a nature that would result in good arrests and swift convictions. So, he waited, but while he waited, he worried.

SAC Richter was a perfect product of the Federal Bureau of Investigation's training. He had been carefully screened, worked his way up the ranks with a good mixture of both administrative and field service, and he was in it to do his job, not to be a hero. This posting was the culmination of a spotless career dealing with wire fraud, mortgage fraud, the occasional bribery investigation, and, when he needed the adrenaline rush, drug trafficking.

But terrorism cases were outside of his experience, and he resented this particular case in particular. The surveillance had shown that the target cell was large, racially diverse, and politically incoherent, and they claimed their weapon was intended to rescue an astronaut. Even if they were incredibly stupid, he found it hard to believe this was their actual motivation, but to his frustration, he couldn't find any alternative.

He had access to briefing papers on Proud Boys and Oath Keepers, on Al Qaeda and ISIS, on Posse Comitatus and the Kurdistan Workers' Party, but he couldn't find anything that covered this and that meant it was new, and when something was new, there was no protocol, no standard operating procedure, no actionable steps; you just had to make it up and hope you didn't get it wrong. In his experience, usually people got it wrong.

SAC Richter's youngest daughter wanted to go to MIT, and that would be overwhelmingly expensive in ten years when she was finally old enough to apply. He needed to keep his job, and more than that, he needed to be promoted if he was ever going to afford her tuition. The last thing he needed was his record blackened this late in the game by some anti-terrorism operation gone wrong. So, overkill and redundancy became his watchwords.

He requested and received a Special Weapons and Tactics Team from Atlanta, and a Hostage Rescue Team and, just in case, a Crisis Negotiation Unit, a fistful of Special Agent Bomb Technicians, and a dozen agents who specialized in Hazardous Devices Operations. Currently, he had them all stashed at the Ramada off I-26.

The agents had all received special training in handling these types of situations and in not touching the minibar, but still, SAC Richter was worried because it had already been a week and having all these specialists there was costing a lot of money, even without anyone downing eight-dollar domestic beers. But he couldn't let them go home yet, because he might need them later.

He was so stressed out that he had started losing his hair. Every morning, he found more of it in his shower drain, and he had started finding his tiny, dark, close-cut hairs sprinkled over his laptop keyboard after his evening email sessions. Some in the FBI would accuse him, later, of requesting too many support agents, but SAC Richter would defend himself by saying that in situations with a great many unknowns, you had to cover all the possibilities.

Were these white-power militants secretly intending to fly their rocket into a building? The tallest building in South Carolina was the Capitol Center, but did they really need a rocket to blow up a twenty-five-story building? Wasn't that overkill? He wished they didn't even have a rocket.

The second they had ordered parts from that Chinese supplier, he had requested permission to move and shut them down, but he had been told to let them get the parts in hand before moving, since it would lead to better arrests. He had asked for written clarification and received it a week after the parts arrived, and of course by then, Washington had changed its mind and issued new orders to stop the delivery. He'd had to explain to them that the parts had been delivered seven days prior to their new directive being issued. He knew they were going to somehow blame him.

At that point, he figured that he should just move in and arrest everyone, but a smooth-talking younger agent who seemed to have powerful mentors in Washington (his father was the Senator from South Carolina) suggested they wait until after the fuel was delivered. SAC Richter hadn't wanted to listen to Special Agent Timmy Ravenel, but the young man did seem to know all the right people, and SAC Richter had good political instincts.

"Man," Timmy Ravenel had said, picking all the cashews out of a bowl of mixed nuts at the hotel bar. "They're never going to get that thing up in the air. It's just a big bomb. As long as we get to it before they put the explosives in, we'll be fine. And the closer they get, the more we look like heroes."

"But what if it explodes prematurely?" John Richter worried. "I don't think any of them are rated for handling dangerous materials."

"Then we've got a bunch of dead dirtbags on our hands," Timmy Ravenel said. "That's a sanitation problem, not a law-enforcement issue. They'll be fertilizer. Reduce, reuse, recycle, right?"

John Richter was doubtful that the motto for the EPA's waste disposal hierarchy was intended to apply to human remains, but he felt that he was so far off the map right now that maybe an entirely different set of laws applied. He hated being off the map. There were no clear guidelines off the map, there was no precedent for this situation, except maybe Waco, and he really didn't think that emulating those command decisions would be good for his career. He was in the dark here, and so he was open to input from anyone who spoke with confidence. Like Timmy Ravenel.

But the budget for the operation kept expanding and his hair kept falling out. He was getting thin at the temples now, but maybe that was just because his bathroom lights were too bright? How many watts were they? A hundred? Seventy-five? Maybe he needed sixties? Either way, the time for action was now, before he was completely bald and right after these domestic terrorists had received their half a million tons of high explosives.

In his defense, he had had no idea it was going to be quite that much. They had purchased it from three different suppliers, and he had really only thought they were buying from one. That was weird, right? Who buys highly explosive materials from three different buyers? What were they, bargain shoppers?

The raid took place at 0500 hours, a time when he believed that most of the camp, and most of the news crews, would be asleep. They hadn't seen anyone except an elderly Caucasian male jogging down the road around 0430 hours followed by a younger male in some kind of cape. The two had jogged right past the FBI rally point, where all the vehicles and men and gear and construction equipment were assembled pre-raid, but SAC Richter had thought that the older gentleman actually looked to be in too much physical pain to notice them, and the one wearing the cape might be mentally handicapped. Who wore a cape in September in South Carolina? The older male did wave, however, which was worrying, but what could one old man with bad knees and a mentally defective boy do against the assembled might of American law enforcement?

Later, during the official inquiry, SAC John Richter would point out that he had twice requested and twice been denied tactical air support, and he believed that this was the hinge on which his failure rested. The investigating committee would point out that his budget was already fifteen times over its original estimate and that his request should have come earlier. In the end, no one was punished and the Director of the FBI issued the following statement: "The Federal Bureau of

Investigation is proud that through their efforts, a terrorist attack on American soil was averted." Which was technically true. They had stopped any terrorism from happening. Mostly because it wasn't going to happen in the first place.

The "go" signal came at 0503 hours. Instantly, two trucks blocked the northbound and southbound approaches to the farm. All target access was now under FBI control. A phalanx of agents, with SWAT in the lead, approached the farm at a brisk jog. There were reports from spotters located inside the treeline behind the farm that a group called Veterans for Peace had made a run for it, along with various underfed nerds, and they estimated that about two hundred people evaporated into the woods before they reached the camp. That was fine with John Richter. He didn't want to have to flashbang any veterans. That always looked bad later.

SWAT was on point in full crowd-control gear, then came the bomb squad, and behind them came field agents in bulletproof vests and FBI windbreakers, jogging two abreast, with bouquets of flexi-cuffs on their belts. Bringing up the rear were five SUVs containing the Crisis Negotiation Unit and other support staff, and then the Hostage Rescue Team, even more heavily armored than SWAT.

The plan was shock and awe: a storming of the farm, immediate seizure of explosives and weapons, followed by an arrest of the leadership and then orders to disperse, backed up by local law enforcement. Already the first problem of the day had reared its head when local law enforcement had shown up at the rally point and the morbidly obese, singularly unprepared police chief had hauled himself out of his vehicle.

"Well, it's like this," he'd drawled in his thick-as-grits upstate accent. "My boys aren't really trained for this kind of situation, and so I feel like it'd be a better idea if we all sort of stay in the back, y'see, so that we're out of your way and avoid obfuscating the engagement."

"I am ordering you to help us serve these warrants," John Richter said.

"Yeah, y'see," the fat man said, "that's just not something we have the tools to handle at the present time. But we won't interfere with you none, so you boys go on and grab the glory. We'll just watch and learn."

It was the first of many things that would go wrong, but SAC Richter didn't let it deter him. His plan was solid: quick tactical penetration, warrants served on leadership and arrests made, explosives secured, buildings emptied, and then they had bulldozers waiting to bring them down. By this time tomorrow morning, SAC Richter figured that the entire camp would be flattened and he could put this incident behind him.

They approached the front gate of the farm at a run, and a splinter of tactical and field agents peeled off from the main body and, like a heavily armored pseudopod, smashed through the front door of the farmhouse. SAC Richter stayed in the main body behind SWAT as they raced ahead towards the gate to the back pasture with its "Redneck NASA" sign spray-painted on a stained bedsheet flapping in the sunrise breeze.

Behind the gate, the fields were a riot of multicolored dome tents, blue plastic tarps, prefabricated buildings, and some dark green military tents, which struck him as practically blasphemous. In the middle of it all was a mass of scaffolding, as delicate as spider webs, surrounding what looked like three huge missiles aimed towards the heavens. Probably duds, SAC Richter figured, but better safe than sorry.

SWAT crashed through the front gate and barreled through the tents like a runaway train. A few early-morning hippies blinked groggily at them from beneath their dreadlocks, but the majority of tents seemed to be empty. Agents tossed tents left and right, moving them out of the way of the SUVs bringing up the rear.

"Go! Go! Go!" SAC Richter screamed pointlessly, because by now all his agents were screaming things that sounded vigorous and proactive, like they'd seen SWAT teams do in hundreds of movies and TV shows.

They angled towards the largest of the buildings, the one that intelligence said contained the control systems. Peeking up over its roof was the enormous outdoor freezer tank containing the explosive materials.

SAC Richter really wished they weren't running directly over the tents, since his agents kept getting tangled up in tension poles and ground cloths, and falling on their hands and knees, but now they were committed. Nothing could stop them.

"SAC Richter?" his earpiece squawked.

"Go for Richter."

"The house is secured. Six individuals detained. One warrant served on a Dr. Paul Rawe."

"Copy that."

They were fifty meters from the control building when they got bogged down. A bunch of space hippies came boiling up out of the tents around them, and the lead SWAT team got mired in them. The rest of the column swung around, but now SAC Richter could see more hippies pouring out of the prefabricated building and coming at them. They were forming a human chain with arms linked at the elbows, and more of them kept materializing, joining the ends of the chain. A second chain formed behind the first, and then a third.

SWAT did their best, but they were trained for quick penetration and takedown, not for dealing with an unwashed chain of half-naked deviants.

"Box it up!" SAC Richter yelled, and the agents formed a defensible position in front of the human chain. Behind them, the SUVs were stuck. One had sucked a drop cloth into its wheel well and the thing had wrapped around its axle. The other four SUVs had tried to drive around it, but one was blocked by hippies clinging to the front bumper, and the other three had gotten clogged with tents, ground cloths, and sleeping bags. They looked like magnets set to attract anything made of nylon within a fifty-foot radius.

John Richter picked up his bullhorn.

"This is Special Agent in Charge John Richter of the FBI. We are here to demand the immediate surrender of Walter Reddie, Paul Rawe, Tiara Flynn, and Patricia 'Big Patty' Campbell. Comply immediately or face arrest."

"We've already got Paul Rawe," a little rat-faced agent whose name he could never remember said from his elbow.

"Scratch Paul Rawe," John said over his bullhorn.

He didn't like the way these human chains were growing. The numbers were against him, but he had better gear and his people had better training than these civilians. Still, speed was of the essence.

"Rubio," he said, addressing the SWAT commander. "Deploy pepper spray and smoke. We've got to secure that control building ASAP."

Rubio shouted something and SWAT pulled on its gas masks. Fire teams dropped back and aimed high with their riot guns, and on the front line big high-pressure cans of pepper spray came out. They started hosing down the human chain who, predictably, fell to the grass, clawing at their eyes and mewling like kittens.

John inhaled a little too deeply and began hacking up mucus. He could feel his sinuses start to thicken and drip.

"Disperse immediately," he said over his bullhorn. "This is an illegal gathering."

Then he nodded to Rubio and hollow bangs sounded across the field as tear-gas canisters arced into the air. A second command and the front line made a baton charge into the human chain, which was only as strong as its many weak links. SWAT put their targets down with blows to the skulls, shoulders, and ribs, leaving them writhing on the ground, moving forward as lightly armored field agents swept in behind them and flexi-cuffed the terrorists, leaving them in the yellow mud churned up by the pepper spray and their own panicked piss.

The morning breeze freshened, blowing ragged clouds of tear gas into his line, but they were wearing gas masks so all it did was obscure some of their observable angles.

"On me!" SAC Richter shouted to several nearby field agents, and a dozen of them formed a flying wedge and speared through the garbage and the tents and closed the last forty meters to the control building.

A shirtless hippie with a beard that John thought had gone out of fashion in the nineteenth century spotted them and yelled, and more of this seemingly inexhaustible supply of filthy people raced to block them. The filth-encrusted losers surrounded the door of the big building and locked arms.

Great, John thought to himself. Good thing he was wearing gloves.

He waded to the big building, his people backhanding obstructors who tried to block their way, but these obstructors were quickly turning into resistors, grabbing FBI arms and belts and taking them to the ground with them. Clots of special agents covered in grungy children toppled over, falling into tents, into grills and portable cookstoves (fire hazards), tripping over extension cords (safety violations) and small children (child abuse). Then John was face-to-face with the shirtless, baroquely bearded nerd.

"FBI. Stand aside."

The geek did exactly what he had hoped he wouldn't do. He laughed.

"Do it!" he cried. "Do it!"

John grabbed a Windex-sized canister of pepper spray from the special agent to his right and he leveled it at the teenager's face. The boy's mouth split into an even bigger grin, and then, in a moment that was vaguely pornographic, he wrapped his lips around the nozzle of the spray. John felt dirty, like he'd been caught with a man's hands down his pants in a public bathroom. He tried to pull his pepper spray back, but the boy bit down on the nozzle and wouldn't let go.

Well, John thought, *you asked for it.*

He depressed the lever and his wrist vibrated as the canister discharged into the boy's mouth. Instantly, the kid dropped to his knees, gagging and retching, gallons of vomit dumping from his throat. Instead of falling face-down, however, he hung in midair, his knees a few inches off the ground, his arms linked on either side to girl nerds. Worse, the girl nerds had linked arms with some more filthy people standing next to them. The gagging nerd dangled, but the chain was unbroken.

"Help me!" John shouted at his agents, who were standing around as if this riot would stop itself. Spurred into action by the anger in his voice, they began ineffectually wrestling with the nerd chain, trying to pull it down. The gagging nerd swung back and forth as the chain jerked and rocked, but it did not break. Then John heard the amplified voice.

"Men and women of the FBI," it brayed.

John looked down to make sure no one had stolen his bullhorn.

"This is Walter Reddie," the voice said.

That got their attention.

"I have with me Tiara Flynn and Big Patty."

The FBI agents had all stopped grappling with their various piles of hippies and were looking for the source of the voice. SAC Richter heard moans and screams around him. He heard the dull *thud, thud, thud* of his men subduing a prone civilian with their batons. Three others struggled with an enormous, shirtless Black man who looked like a teenager grown to the size of a refrigerator. He kept shoving into them like a linebacker, dripping with yellow pepper spray, the agents trying to hold him slipping and sliding in the mud.

"Martin," the amplified voice said, addressing the fat man. "Stop fighting. You don't want to get arrested."

Martin either didn't hear or he ignored what he heard. Now he was crushing a young female FBI agent against one of the SUVs with his massive, naked belly.

"Martin," the voice of Walter Reddie echoed. "Come on, everyone's watching you."

His orders were ignored. An agent pulled out a taser and dropped Martin to the ground. SWAT approached, taking their batons off their belt.

"Hold up," Walter Reddie's voice said. "Martin's not a bad guy; he's just passionate. We're all passionate."

John saw the whiskery, elderly jogger who had passed him on the road earlier that morning clinging to the scaffolding that surrounded the missiles, about six meters off the ground. That was Walter Reddie? He felt frustrated that he could have arrested him half an hour before with no fuss. Now he held up his fist and the SWAT approaching the boy stood by. Just in case there were cameras. You didn't want to get caught on camera doing something like that. It never looked good.

"We're not terrorists," Reddie said. "We're men and women building a spacecraft to go to the International

Space Station. I know what we're doing isn't strictly legal, but if we don't go rescue my cousin, who will?"

John gestured to two agents to follow him towards the scaffolding, but they weren't paying attention. They were listening to Reddie. Great. He made a note of their names so he could write them up in his report later. He caught the attention of a third, and the two of them began picking their way over.

"We're responsible to a higher power here," Walter Reddie continued on his bullhorn. "We're going into space. This is what human beings were made to do! People of the FBI, don't give yourself over to brutes, don't surrender your humanity to a cold machine. Join us, work with us. Think for yourselves.

"Who are we hurting here? Don't be machines serving the one percent; be men serving the ninety-nine percent. How can you bring yourselves to hurt these people? These people who could be your sons or your daughters, your brothers or your sisters. We have grandparents here, grandmothers and grandfathers. Join us, join us and help us take humanity to the stars!"

The crowd was riveted by Reddie. Hanging on his every word. SAC Richter took in Reddie hanging from the scaffolding by one arm, directly above him like a pirate dangling from the rigging of his ship with a bullhorn in one hand. He cut a dashing figure against the sky: craggy, heroic, noble. It was a beautiful moment. Richter tased him.

"Uuuuuguuuguuuuuguuu," Reddie yelled through

the bullhorn, and then he dropped bonelessly to the ground like a sack full of cow shit.

By 0700 hours, all four warrants were served, all four suspects were in custody, and all of the dangerous materials were secured. By 0800, SAC Richter felt a hell of a lot better. The first news crew had just been stopped at the roadblock and were setting up on the shoulder, but by now the situation was well in hand and he was confident that while his superiors might nitpick a few details here and there, it wasn't going to adversely affect his permanent record. Plus, any footage that was being shot made this look like a well-organized success. Mission accomplished.

There were so many people arrested that it took them hours to get enough transport for them. The final count was forty-two arrestees, including the four on SAC Richter's shopping list. He couldn't wait to call DC and let them know that the situation was well in hand.

Lots of cuts and bruises, a bunch of kids with burning eyes who would think twice before disobeying a command from law enforcement again, and one dislocated shoulder from a too-vigorous flexi-cuffing incident. He heard about people needing stitches and complaints of concussions and skull fractures, but he'd believe those diagnoses when a doctor confirmed them. Now all they were faced with was a carpool problem.

"We've got some seats opening up in the minivans," Timmy Ravenel said.

"How many?" SAC Richter asked.

"About twenty-five agents are staying behind to secure the explosives, so that's twenty-five seats free for the ride down."

"Fine," SAC Richter said. "But I want Reddie with me."

He regretted that decision after he slid into the front seat of his SUV. He checked his shoes.

"Is that you?" he asked his driver. His driver jerked a thumb over his shoulder.

SAC Richter turned around in his seat and saw the miserable Walter Reddie. He looked even more like a derelict up close, and the man smelled. Bad.

"Don't you people shower?" SAC Richter asked.

"Sorry," Reddie rasped. "Been busy."

"It just seems to me that if you're serious about going into space, you might provide your people with bathroom facilities."

The SUV pulled out and behind it trailed a convoy of FBI vehicles bouncing over the dirt driveway and down to the hard-surface road. The eighteen-wheelers blocking the southern approach to the highway pulled aside to let them pass.

"What about... my house?" Reddie managed before a coughing fit overcame him.

"Impounded," SAC Richter said. "Along with anything we find out here. South Carolina's a civil-forfeiture state, so everything your terrorist cell owned now belongs to the people."

"Not… terrorists," Reddie coughed.

"That's a matter of perspective," SAC Richter said.

The double *BANGs* were loud and they sent the SUV slewing to its right, dropping low like its wheels had come off their axles, throwing SAC Richter into his window, skull first. He felt something snap in his right shoulder.

"Shit! Shit! Shit!" his driver shouted.

He smelled burning rubber and scorching brake pads as his SUV fishtailed to a stop. Something shoved them hard from behind, and he turned to see the SUV behind them crack their back windshield and stop. It kept him from seeing farther back down the road.

In his side-view mirror he saw the two SUVs behind him halted, parked at odd angles. He pushed his door open with his left arm and got out to establish a visual, and a searing pain drove through the ball of his right foot and he dropped to one knee.

"Jesus Christ!" he shouted.

Down near the surface of the road, he got a good view of them: nails bent around another nail to form black iron triangles, scattered across the asphalt from one side to the other. They hung from the front tire of his SUV like ticks. Terrified, he turned over his right foot and saw one embedded halfway through the sole of his shoe.

"We need support and Medevac—" he shouted at his driver, and then a roar like the ocean crashed over his SUV from the left.

He hauled himself up on one foot, holding onto the door for support and saw a host of hippies with red, watering eyes, naked torsos covered in bruises, pouring out of the trees bordering the two-lane blacktop. There were hundreds of them, maybe thousands, and they were hooting and hollering and running right at the immobilized convoy. Their front line carried push brooms. As soon as they reached the road they began sweeping the nails forward and away.

He swung himself back into his seat, ignoring the burning pain in his right foot, pulling his door closed.

"Lock the—" Richter shouted, and then they were upon them.

Hands slapped the body of the car, T-shirts and man-nipples and beer bellies were pressed to the windows, people climbed onto the hood and roof and jumped up and down. All of the FBI's gear, all of their training, all of their nonlethal weaponry, none of it meant anything because they couldn't even get out of their vehicles and their vehicles were sitting on their rims.

The crush of bodies kept them from opening their doors; the roar of the crowd kept them from hearing each other on their earpieces. They were blind and deaf. SAC Richter thought he told his driver to draw his sidearm, but either the man didn't hear him or he wasn't about to fire into a wall of human beings.

The door handles were going *KLUNKA-KLUNKA-KLUNKA* as people outside the cars worked them frantically back and forth and, unable to gain access, tennis-shoed feet started kicking in the windshield.

"Don't!" John shouted, as visions of legs punching through the safety glass and smashing into his face danced through his head. "Stop!"

But the feet kept kicking the glass. SAC Richter hit the power-window button and rolled it down, then he rolled all the windows down. He had no choice. The glass would be smashed if he didn't let them in, and their bodies were jammed too tight against the doors to open them.

The noise of the crowd jumped fifty decibels as the windows opened and a forest of hands reached into the car. A girl with a nose ring squirmed into the backseat, pulled out a Leatherman, and clipped Reddie's flexi-cuffs. John lifted his cell phone to take her picture.

She just laughed and plucked the phone out of his hand, slid open the back, and plucked out his SIM card.

"That's government property!" he yelled, but she was already being pulled back out of the window, laughing as she disappeared. As they pulled him away, Reddie put one horny and callused hand on John's shoulder.

"Don't come back," he said.

Then he was sucked away by the crowd churning outside, and then they were retreating into the trees, and then the road was empty, and the birds were singing again, and SAC Richter could hear the cheers and victorious shouts floating to him from far away. His driver listened to his earpiece and then turned to him.

"That was Agent Casey up at the farm. He says they were just evicted. He says they used 'hugging.' I'm not exactly sure what he means."

"Shut. Up," SAC Richter said.

The driver shut up. SAC Richter pressed the heels of his hands into his eyes, then he pounded the dashboard.

"Shit!" he yelled. "Shit! Shit! Shit! We're going to have another Waco."

"We are not going to have another Waco," Walter Reddie said from the head of the table.

They had crowded into the wreckage of his house, everyone who could fit. They walked over kicked-down doors, stepped around broken glass, and picked up toppled shelves to get down the hall. Now they were jammed into the kitchen, arguing, debating, panicking, trying to figure out how to keep the FBI from coming back and taking away the only thing they had left: *Space Jesus*.

"How'd you get rid of the ones they left up here?" Reddie asked Volor.

"Glomping," Volor said, proudly.

"Do I even want to know?" Walter asked.

"It's an unbeatable battlefield strategy," Volor said. "They only left about forty behind, so I found everyone who'd ever been to an anime convention and made them Glomp Leaders. Glomping is like when you see someone who makes you squee and you run up and you give them a really tight hug and you don't let go. Each of the Glomp Leaders got a team of twenty and taught them how to glomp, and then each team targeted a cop, ran over, and glomped the hell out of them."

"Sweet Jesus," Walter sighed.

"They were totally immobilized. Have you ever tried to do anything with twenty people hugging you at once?" Volor gave a high-pitched laugh. He was jacked up on adrenaline. "It feels good, but it's impossible to escape that kind of cuddle pile. We just picked each of them up in the middle of the glomp cluster and walked them off the farm. They can't stop the glomp!"

"No," Walter said. "They can't. But they can come back and bulldoze us. They could bring up water cannons and tear down this camp. Blast 'Achy Breaky Heart' over and over again at two o'clock in the morning until our eardrums bleed and we beg for mercy. That's what they can do."

"They called me a terrorist," Paul said, numbly. He'd never even gotten a parking ticket before. "I'm never going to get a job again."

Tiara was almost catatonic, clutching Bathsheba at

the end of the table. The little girl was red-eyed and sniffling. She'd gotten tear gas in the face, not a lot but it had taken a long time to flush her eyes and get her to stop crying. The fact that her mother had been arrested in front of her hadn't helped.

"There's only one thing we can do," Walt said. "We've got to stop."

"But we won!" Volor said.

"They're going to come back and they're going to come back in force. We gotta stop before more people get hurt."

That's when the shouting broke out. Everyone wanted to talk at once, so they all had to escalate their voices over each other to be heard, getting louder and louder until the room was vibrating with anger, recriminations, and accusations. The only people not talking were the people being talked at: Tiara, Paul, and Walter. And then:

SMASH!

Someone threw a chair through the one unbroken window left in the room. Everyone froze, thinking the FBI was back, but it was Paul's wife, Lynne. She stood in front of the shattered window, hands curled into fists, face bright red.

"Are you kidding me?" she asked.

"Honey," Paul said. "You don't understand what's—"

"I came here," Lynne said, "because I was sick and tired of living with a quitter. And now you're all quitting? Those people out there aren't going to let you quit. You surrender and there is going to be a riot. This whole place will fall apart."

"This isn't the time for you to finally start being political," Walter said. "We got injuries all over the place. We resisted arrest. They aren't going to let us launch."

"When did you start caring about what a bunch of assholes in windbreakers would or would not let you do?" Lynne asked.

"Lynne..." Paul began.

"Don't say my name in that tone of voice," she snapped. "If I wanted to hear a little girl whine, I would have given birth to one. You're in it now. You guys are all in it up to the tops of your heads and it's too late to quit. You stop now and you're terrorists. You launch that rocket and you're astronauts. Don't you think a bunch of astronauts stand a better chance in court than a bunch of terrorists?"

"Even if we move the launch date up," Walter said. "Even if we're able to get *Space Jesus* ready to launch this coming Friday, how do we keep the FBI from just storming in and arresting every single one of us? That'll be a danger right up until the very last second of the launch. You're so fired up, Lynne, then tell me, what are you going to do about that?"

"You dumbass hick," Lynne said. "You let me worry about that. I've got a brain."

"Now, honey, that's—" Paul began, but his wife ignored him.

"Memomma," she asked. "I need you to find a whole bunch of dangerous grannies for me. Can you do that?"

"I reckon so..." Memomma said.

"How many children are here?" Lynne asked. "A few? A lot?"

"Lynne, what are you talking about?" Paul whined.

"Stop being such a turn-off, Paul," she said. "How many kids are here?"

"I think there's, like, fifty or something," Tiara said. "Like, maybe that many?"

"Good," Lynne said. "Get them all and follow me."

When John Richter had been nine years old, his daddy bought him a bicycle. He didn't know how to ride it, but his daddy's approach was learning by doing. The first time he tried to ride it, he fell off. He'd wanted to quit. His daddy had yelled at him until he got back on the bike, and he promptly fell off again.

More yelling. Another attempt. Another failure. On his twelfth try, he fell off and hit his head on the driveway and had to be taken to the emergency room, blood streaming down his face. He'd gotten five stitches.

Two weeks later, they took the stitches out, and then, with his daddy's encouragement, he got back on the bike and this time he was able to make it to the end of the driveway. Now, twenty-two years later, the scar at his hairline was barely visible and he knew how to ride a bike. John Richter had learned a valuable lesson from his daddy that day: always get back on the horse that threw you.

He sent agents to all the rental-car agencies within driving distance and they put down government plastic and snapped up every minivan they could find. He didn't listen to protests, he ignored his email, he didn't answer his cell phone. He sent in SWAT to clear the road of every single anti-tire device and had Agent Ravenel add more charges to the warrants.

Now, five hours later, they were back at the rally point. They'd go in bulldozer-first this time, and if the press filmed them and made them look like thugs, so be it. He was not going to see his career go down in flames, taking his daughter's MIT dreams with it, because a bunch of homeless terrorists thought they could launch a missile in Melville, SC, on his watch. The situation was still salvageable. He just had to get back on the horse that threw him.

"Sir, I think you need to come see this," the rat-faced special agent said.

SAC Richter was debating bulldozer deployment with SWAT Captain Rubio. He knew more tactical units were being deployed from North Carolina, Georgia, and Tennessee, but he needed to handle this now, before they got there. Come nightfall, he was going to come down on these hillbillies like the hammer of God.

"What is it?"

The rat-faced agent was part of the forward observation unit who'd been sent to scout the encampment. They were supposed to find the best point for penetration, not come running back to him like a bunch of crybabies.

"It's… I just think you'd better see for yourself."

Annoyed, SAC Richter limped after the young agent up the road to the turn-off to the farm. They crouched low and limp-ran forward to the stand of pine trees at the top of the rise where the observation unit had set up post. John knelt down in the pine needles next to three agents and snatched a pair of field glasses from one of them.

"What am I looking for?" he asked.

"A day care center," the agent said.

SAC Richter had no idea what the man was talking about and then, suddenly, he did. At first, it looked like child's birthday party in the middle of the road with balloons and streamers and big pads of paper tied to the split-rail fence. Then SAC Richter realized that there were children all over, playing games, sitting for story time, singing songs, playing recorder. He counted close to fifty of them, they were clearly enjoying themselves, and they were all over the dirt road to the farm.

Leading them in their games were elderly women, about a dozen of them, and then he saw that there were more of these old ladies all around the perimeter of the daycare. They were sitting in lawn chairs and chatting, doing word jumbles and cross-stitch, flipping through *Reader's Digest*, fanning themselves, and playing cards. One had an extension cord hooked up and was watching TV. And all of them were blocking access to the farm.

One of the other agents turned to him in horror. His face said it all.

"Sir," he said, aghast. "Please tell me we don't have to pepper-spray our moms."

SAC John Richter's plans were toast.

The camp had already been too large and unwieldy to hold together for much longer, and now it was trapped inside a cordon of FBI agents, sealed off from the world, and the pressure was mounting. The FBI had blocked the road and surrounded the farm on all sides so no one could get in or out.

Most of the press had been staying in town where they could get hot showers, except for one poor sap from the *Huffington Post*, and now they were all corralled in the FBI press pen down by the highway, and no matter how much they begged, pleaded, argued, or shouted, they weren't getting through.

The cordon was a double-edged sword. On the one hand, the only access to Redneck NASA was through the front gate, and no one in law enforcement was willing to tear-gas a bunch of old grannies and small children. They wouldn't even let rip with a late-night, high-decibel rendition of "My Heart Will Go On" as long as they thought it might traumatize the kids.

On the other hand, nothing the camp needed was getting in. Walt had a well, so there was plenty of water, and they had mostly been running on generators before the raid anyways, but food was running out fast.

Miss Adele and Miss Fisher's stockpiles had been torn to pieces by the FBI, trampled to mush. What little they'd salvaged would be sucked down the insatiable maw of the Rocket Zombies in a matter of days. They couldn't keep working at this breakneck pace while suffering calorie cuts at the same time. It was impossible.

But the Rocket Zombies kept going. They felt unbeatable. They were three thousand strong. What could possibly stop them now? In the face of their strength, the FBI looked like people seen from far up in the sky: puny, small, ignorant. Like ants. But the clock was ticking. They had to launch.

Walter and Tiara sat on the roof of Walt's mostly destroyed house and listened to the town meeting down in his yard. Paul conducted it over a bullhorn.

"I know you're tired, but by now you all have your work assignments," he bellowed. "Anyone not have a work assignment? If so, please go to Memomma's office right now."

A few people drifted off. The meeting moved on. They were T minus eighteen hours and holding. Everyone was moving on fast-forward except Walter, who was being pulled away from the whirlwind of activity so he could come to terms with what was going to happen with him in less than a day.

"Don't you think we should ask people to move further away?" Tiara asked. "They're all way too close to the launchpad. I think?"

"Where're they gonna go?" Walt asked. "Now that we're penned up in here, there's no place to spread out. Besides, we've said it a dozen times already: move the hell back. There comes a point when warning people who aren't listening ain't much different than talking to yourself."

"Tomorrow morning," Paul continued, bellowing over the bullhorn to the thousands on the farm as well as the hundreds of representatives of the FBI, the ATF, and the FAA spread out around them, "*Space Jesus* will launch. She's got to be going seven miles per second straight up, and about four minutes after liftoff, we're going to lose communication with her. That's when she's going to turn horizontal to the ground.

"Once she's about six minutes into her flight, she's going to enter a transfer orbit, which is where we adjust her trajectory to about fifty-one point six degrees of inclination and circularize her orbit so that she's on an intercept course to the ISS. We'll only get one chance to intercept the space station, because she can't carry any more fuel weight to readjust her course if she misses. After she comes out of transfer orbit, we have one chance to put her on a single orbital trajectory that'll intercept the ISS. But she's going to do it. Because we are capable of anything. Anything!"

A cheer went up.

"You know," Walt said, "I could use a drink."

"I'm not launching you drunk," Tiara said.

"Who're you to tell me what I can and can't do?"

"Do you really want to be drunk the first time you actually go into space?"

"Yeah, well," Walt said. "I've just had some time to think. Once you rub off all the fancy parts, I am essentially standing in a phone booth with three hundred tons of high explosives up my ass, aiming to hit the equivalent of a tennis ball floating on the Atlantic Ocean based on calculations performed by a pack of hillbillies who think professional wrestling is real."

Tiara thought about it for a minute.

"What's a phone booth?" she asked.

Later that night, Walt couldn't sleep, and so he crawled out onto the roof again. It was the one place where no one would talk to him. Up above stretched the stars, spread across the night sky. Below him, a massive line of people stretched across the camp. They were all tired, worn out, asleep on their feet. The tail of the line wrapped around itself several times, but its head rested at the base of *Space Jesus*.

One by one, the people in line shuffled forward and when they got close to *Space Jesus*, they laid their hands on her skin. Some of them prayed. Some of them pressed their foreheads to her cold steel. Others kissed her. Then they moved on, revitalized. This was the closest any of them would ever come to space. They had built *Space Jesus*. She was theirs. And they were going to launch her to the stars at sunrise.

Walter started getting scared.

Launch day dawned bright and mostly clear. After the Space Shuttle *Atlantis* got struck by lightning in 1986, stringent launch conditions were imposed by NASA. They wouldn't tolerate any weather interference whatsoever, they wouldn't tolerate storms, they wouldn't even tolerate clouds within five miles. But Redneck NASA was doing it Soviet-style. The Russians launched in snowstorms, they launched in hailstorms, and they launched in high winds that would ground most commercial aircraft. They didn't give a fuck; they just wanted to get into space, no matter what it cost.

This morning, there were some clouds in the sky,

rumors of rain in the afternoon, a light breeze blowing from the southwest; it was enough to scrub a NASA mission, but it wasn't going to stop *Space Jesus*. For Redneck NASA, this was well within acceptable margins.

Teams had been working around the clock, fueling the three massive rockets that made up the launch vehicle. With limited room to move people back from the launchpad, fire teams had dug blast trenches and diverter walls to shield some of the farm from the exhaust of the massive engines, but no one was exactly sure how things were going to shake out once the torch was lit. But Walter, sitting on the edge of his bed in a cold sweat, knew exactly how things would go.

Rockets function entirely on the principle that gases flow from a high-pressure environment to a low-pressure environment until the pressure in both environments is equal. So, first, the massive, pressurized tanks of liquid oxygen at the top of the boosters would be activated. The tanks would open and the LOX would race through a nozzle at the base of the fuel chamber and surge towards the lower-pressure solid-fuel chamber, passing over a pyrograin in the process, which would cause it to explode.

The burning oxygen would shower the inside of the solid-fuel chamber, turning it into a holocaust of fire that would ignite the polyurethane rods. They would vaporize instantly and send hot gases racing to the nearest low-pressure environment: outside.

Between the hundreds of tons of roiling molten gas and the outside lay the nozzle, which would accelerate the exhaust by choking it, pushing it to an even higher speed that would break the sound barrier, turning the gases into a jet, converting their thermal energy into kinetic energy, and shoving the half-million pounds of *Space Jesus* into the sky faster than a bullet fired from a gun.

Space Jesus would punch through the troposphere, the stratosphere, the mesosphere, and then it would enter the thermosphere, just past the one-hundred-kilometer Kármán line. In those first six minutes of flight, she would use up all one point five million pounds of fuel. After that, Walt would be in the hands of God, or physics, which were the same thing as far as he was concerned.

He needed a drink.

Fortunately for him, Volor's mom must have been a lazy-ass alcoholic, because the kid hadn't found the fifth he kept hidden in the tank of his toilet. Walt poured himself a waterglass-full and tossed it back. It tasted like heaven after being vodka-free for almost a month. He felt like he'd sweated years of vodka out of his system, leaving a vacancy for more vodka to fill him back up again, and that's all he was doing: replacing what he'd lost. Because he was scared. This might be his last morning alive. He didn't want to meet his maker without his vodka levels topped up. He polished off the rest of the fifth and then slid the bottle underneath his mattress.

He rinsed his mouth out with toothpaste, and, moving free and easy, he left his house and walked, loose-limbed and limber, across the farm and into the barn. The launch crew swarmed around him, fitting his Commie trash bag, handing him his helmet. Paul helped him fit his catheter, and then Tiara pulled him aside.

"You're drunk."

"I had a drink," Walter said. "Yes."

"You promised," she said.

"You're not going to cry, are you? It was just a little vodka."

"You promised," she said.

"Promises were made to be broken."

She stalked off. Paul had overheard everything and he shook his head.

"Sober or not, you have to go up. We can't hold," he said.

"Wouldn't want it any other way," Walt said.

Except he slurred *other* and it came out "udder."

Since he weighed an extra eighty pounds with the Commie trash bag, and no one wanted to see him trip and bust a kneecap on his way to *Space Jesus*, they loaded Walt onto a hand truck and hauled him outside, standing straight, clasping his helmet to his stomach with both arms. Suddenly, it felt real to him, like he was back at Canaveral getting ready to board. His balls began to sweat.

Everyone stopped what they were doing and began

to clap as he passed, which turned into cheering, which woke up the FBI, who started snapping pictures with their monstrous telephoto lenses. The press saw the FBI taking pictures and they began to film, and then they all realized that it was really happening, and anchors got their makeup done, producers got on their cell phones, SWAT fingered their weapons.

Walt refused to act like some sort of monkey on parade and wave. He just kept his eyes straight ahead as they wheeled him to *Space Jesus*. At the base of the rockets, a harness was locked around his chest. It was attached to a chain, and they hoisted him one hundred feet straight up into the air.

Three workers on top of the scaffold pulled him in and unsnapped the chain. Gripping him under the arms, they lowered him into the nose cone of *Space Jesus* and strapped him down.

Then they waited. The three techs dangled their legs over the edge of the platform, occasionally speaking or double-checking their lists. A bird trilled something from down in the pines, and Walt almost forgot that he was perched on top of a mountain of high explosives, waiting for them to be lit.

From up there it all looked so peaceful, like something laid out on a map. There was the launchpad with the thousands of tents around it, hundreds of sleeping bags, thousands of people. Then there was the barn, Mission Control, the house where he had grown up, and beyond that the fence and the daycare, then the FBI and the cops, the media behind them, and then the road leading to the rest of the country. It all looked so neat and orderly from one hundred feet in the sky.

Over on the roof of Mission Control, Anne Templeton waved her semaphore flags. It was the Go signal.

"Time to fly, Walt," one of the techs said.

"Reckon so," Walt answered. He was sobering up fast.

They put his helmet on and secured the locks around the bottom of his yoke collar, shutting out the sound of the birds and the wind. They lowered the clear dome over the end of *Space Jesus* and bolted it down with screw guns. Now Walter was locked inside the ship, locked inside his suit. There was no turning back. He was going to be fired off this planet like a bullet, into cold, unforgiving space. It was silent in there, doubly sealed off from the world, and he could hear nothing but a hollow ringing in his ears. He was all alone with his fear.

Inside, Mission Control was buzzing with quiet purpose, intense focus, and massive concentration. Paul wondered if this was how it felt in real life. He'd designed rockets but never launched one. Not into space. He felt like he was part of a select fraternity of human beings, the few men and women who'd sent a member of their species off this planet. He bet that all of them put together, that everyone who had ever launched a rocket, couldn't even fill a small stadium.

Near him, Tiara smacked gum and listened intently to her headset. She'd had a friend put her hair in braids for today, and they made her look focused and ready for action. She radioed Walt to make sure his comm equipment was working.

"Good to go," he said on the open channel. Paul could detect a barely controlled hitch in his voice. He knew Walter had been drinking, but he wasn't sure what this undertone of panic was. The beginning of a breakdown? The start of a slide into uncontrolled terror?

"Tiara," he said, offline. "Ask him if he's okay."

"Walter, are you doing okay?" Tiara asked, all quiet concern.

"Yes… no," Walter said, his voice echoing from the speaker system.

Paul checked the closed-circuit cameras. Outside, people were being herded away by the Goon Squad, pressed as far as possible from the launchpad, leaving behind abandoned tents and ground cloths.

Then Walter said:

"I want to come in."

Everyone froze. They looked up at the speaker near the ceiling as if studying a face for clues.

"Come again?" Tiara asked.

"I want to come in," Walter repeated, sounding slightly surer of himself. "This isn't a good idea. I've got some system irregularities in the pumping mechanism."

Paul checked his screens.

"I'm showing all clear," he told Tiara.

"We're not showing any irregularities on our side," Tiara said.

"You need to abort the launch and check them out," Walter said, suddenly sounding very scared.

"We can't abort, Tiara," Paul told her offmic. "It's too late."

She didn't say anything. She looked at Paul, then she looked at her screens, pressing the headset tighter to the side of her head with one hand.

"Please," Walter begged, his voice taking on the garble of the panic bargainer. "I'm scared and I'm drunk. I never should have had that vodka. I'm seeing double now, I can't focus. I take it back. I don't want to do this. I was wrong. There's too many things that could go wrong. I don't want to do this. Don't send me into space. Please. I'm begging you."

Tiara sat, frozen.

"You have to do something," Paul hissed at her in a panic.

"Please," Walter begged. "For the love of God."

Tiara sat up straight; she tapped one of her screens and toggled the intercom.

"Initiate countdown," she said.

"Don't do this to me," Walter gabbled.

Tiara switched his comms off the main speakers, so now it was only coming in over headsets.

"Arm launch vehicle and clear the tower," she said, her voice on all channels, on all speakers, echoing over the farm. "We are launch commit."

"You're killing me," Walter Reddie screamed. And then they heard him doing something new. It took them almost twenty seconds to realize he was crying. "I don't want to go into space. I want to go home."

"All personnel, please clear the launchpad, please clear the blast zone," Tiara said, loud and clear.

"I'm going to die up there," Walter sobbed. "You're killing me. You're sending me to die."

"Transfer from ground to internal power," Tiara said. "Visors locked, sunglasses on if you're watching the launch, we are at fifteen."

"You're murdering me," Walter sobbed over their headsets.

"Tiara…" Paul said.

Tears ran down her face but she brushed them away angrily on her sleeve.

"We are at ten," she said, struggling to keep her voice steady.

"Tiara…" Paul repeated.

The countdown reached zero.

"Light the fire," Tiara said.

Then she pressed Ignite and Walter Reddie was shot into space, screaming in fear and pissing his pants.

* * *

Out on the launchpad, "Zero" echoed in the air. No one knew what to expect. Then it came. At first, there was a silent billow of smoke that rose up out of the Father, the Son, and the Holy Ghost, rolling across the ground like tear gas, shockingly white and thick, like cotton. It was the polyurethane baking, not yet hot enough to form a jet. Then, suddenly there was a spark and then fire and then the bass hiss of the flame. *Space Jesus* sat still for a minute until, suddenly, it didn't and it was like God reached down and plucked it up into the sky.

Fire rolled across the ground like water, vaporizing nylon tents and melting the tarps where it touched them. Boiling hot smoke rolled across the crowd, pressed all the way back against the FBI cordon. Everyone's heads went back as one, and they all watched *Space Jesus* lift into the sky, and then its contrails curved gracefully and cut a perfect arc across the bright blue vault of the heavens.

The Rocket Zombies were crying. They never thought they'd see this moment. Some were burned badly, but they didn't feel it yet. Inside Mission Control, the Big Brains were jumping up and down and cheering like they'd lost their minds.

First one, and then three, and then dozens of FBI agents took off their combat helmets, and they told themselves it was just to keep them from falling off backwards as they strained their heads back to see the rocket fly.

Norbert watched his work fly, and it was better than any sex he had ever had, Big Patty was terrified by the overwhelming noise and screamed, Uncle AJ popped open his first beer of the day and raised it in a toast to his nephew, SAC John Richter stood with his mouth hanging open and he felt like a little boy again, Volor covered his best friend with his body so she wouldn't get scalded by the smoke. And all the grannies, and the rednecks, and the Rocket Zombies, and the fools, and the freeloaders, and the freaks, and the cops, and the cameramen, and the makeup artists, and the news anchors watched in silence as one of their own went soaring into space.

"Well, I'll be," Huggies said. "Those idiots actually made the damn thing fly."

Mr. Gaudy had been the official spokesman of Melville during the standoff, so it made sense that he'd be the one to address the press. It didn't mean that he wanted to do it, but his entire career as an educator had consisted of doing nothing but things he didn't want to do, so this came natural to him. He was practicing his statement when Huggies came into the locker room bathroom and gave him the bad news.

"We just made radio contact," Huggies said.

"Radio contact?" Mr. Gaudy asked.

"Turns out that he's not dead. What are you doing?"

"I'm practicing my speech."

"To the toilet?"

"Whom do you suggest?"

"You can practice on me."

"Well, obviously I'll have to rewrite it now."

He had already prepared a speech about sacrifice and the way it brought small American towns—like this one—full of good, American people—like these—closer together. But knowing that Walter Reddie was still alive, and probably suffering from the DTs, somewhere up in space made the entire thing unusable.

"No time for rewrites," Huggies said. "The whole world wants to hear what you have to say."

"Now?"

"Absolutely now."

Mr. Gaudy looked like he might throw up.

"Relax, buddy," Huggies said. "That makeup gal did you all pretty. You're going to be a star."

What he meant to say was *Better you than me*.

He led Mr. Gaudy to the locker-room door and patted him on the shoulder.

"Make Melville proud."

Then he opened the door to the gym. The school district had been convinced to reopen it solely for this press conference. They needed the room because everyone was there; the entire country, it seemed to Mr. Gaudy. Normally, that would have flattered his vanity, but today it just made his mouth dry.

Huggies pushed Mr. Gaudy out like a cow onto the killing floor, steering him with both hands on his shoulders. Mr. Gaudy's feet were numb and swollen. Flashbulbs blinded him; shutters clicked like angry insects all around and drowned out any other sound. He inched to the portable stage, shouldering his way through the crush of people, keeping his eyes down so he didn't run the risk of meeting all their eyes.

He took the high step to the stage, and the room went quiet. The entire press corps of the United States of America squeezed in front, and the whole population of Melville, SC, packed in all around their backs, spilling out the doors, standing on the bleachers, hanging from the backboards. Everyone was waiting for him to speak. He stepped to the podium and took out his papers. Flashbulbs flickered like heat lightning.

"Ladies and gentlemen," he said and they hung on his every word. *Ladies and gentlemen*, that was right, wasn't it? "Ladies and gentlemen, thank you for joining us today—"

"What's the update?" a reporter shouted.

"Is anyone being prosecuted for terrorism?" another screamed.

Chaos erupted as the reporters all started jabbering at once, a heaving ocean of confusion and noise from the floor, lapping at his chest, threatening to drown him. Mr. Gaudy looked around helplessly, his eyes rolling wildly.

"Please…" he said. "Please…"

No one listened.

Then a mighty sword of fire sliced through the confusion. A huge blast of sound that brutalized everyone into submission, a noise that sounded like the end of the world. As the crowd fell silent, Mr. Gaudy saw that it was Jimmy Royal in his wheelchair, holding up two air horns. He had his thumbs on their buttons and he didn't let up until everyone was grimacing in pain, hands clamped over their ears. Just when Mr. Gaudy was considering begging Sheriff Bennet to shoot Jimmy to make that horrible noise stop, Jimmy lifted his thumbs.

"Thank you, James," Mr. Gaudy said, struggling to regain his composure, his ears ringing. "As I was saying, ladies and gentlemen, thank you all for joining us today. This morning, we confirmed the status of the vehicle known as '*Space Jesus,*' which was launched from the encampment known as 'Redneck NASA.'" He wanted to make sure they understood his distaste for those names. He wanted them to hear the air quotes in his voice. "We have also confirmed that shortly after intercepting the International Space Station, '*Space Jesus*' suffered critical problems with hull integrity and broke apart in orbit. Walter Reddie is on board the International Space Station with minor injuries, but there is no way for him to return."

Camera shutters clicked, reporters murmured into their recording devices, zoom lenses telescoped in close to see if they could catch a tear slithering down Mr. Gaudy's pale cheek, but his face was disappointingly dry.

"The mission has failed," he said.

Disappointed cries came from the citizens of Melville pressed back against the gymnasium walls. Miss Adele put her arms around Jimmy Ferguson and held him while he wept. Terry Thurman wiped angrily at his face. A boy in high-heeled boots and eyeliner punched the bleachers, injuring his hand. And the press kept staring at Mr. Gaudy, waiting for what he was going to say next.

All this concentrated attention pushed Mr. Gaudy to a higher state of consciousness. He felt like someone else, looking down on himself looking out over the gym. Everyone looked so bright and detailed, as if he'd just taken off a pair of sunglasses he'd been wearing all his life. He could see them all so clearly now.

Mrs. Huggins, hands clenched over her chest, wasn't the mayor's obnoxious, pushy wife. She was a member of the team in charge of parachute production. Oddie Beaufort was shaking his head sadly, looking down at the floor, no longer a potbellied drunk with the manners of a pig but the fellow who had built most of the blast trenches.

Mr. Gaudy looked over at Tiara Flynn, testing his new vision. She was standing under the electronic scoreboard, eyes swollen from crying, holding her daughter to her chest, and he didn't see the school slut with fake hair and stonewashed jeans. He saw an aeronautics engineer. Doby Cleckley was picking at his face, looking dumbstruck, not some failure who had moved back home because he couldn't hack it in the real world, but the assistant to the engineer who had designed the rockets.

Clumped together at the end of the bleachers, Mr. Gaudy didn't see a washed-up football team who would never make it to state finals no matter how hard they tried. He saw a fire-control team who had put out three serious blazes when the rocket launched. Over by the wall, those weren't unemployed pipefitters; they were avionics engineers.

For once, the gym of Ron McNair High School wasn't a temporary holding pen for unemployable heathens and redneck troublemakers who were going nowhere fast. Today, it was full of physicists and engineers, materials specialists and systems analysts. They were flight directors, mold makers, pyrotechnicians, firefighters, computer programmers, recovery-team divers, rocket welders.

These people had finally found a purpose in their lives, they had finally found something to believe in, and it had been almost immediately snatched away. That was the hard truth that hung over them all this morning. They had tried, and they had failed. The world didn't see them as astronauts; it saw them as failures.

And in that instant, like he was touched by the hand of God, Mr. Gaudy knew what he had to do. He knew what had to say. For too many years, he had gone through the motions. For too many years, he had hated these people because of the tiny world they forced him to inhabit. But now he saw that he was the only one who could save them. He leaned into the microphone.

"Before I came out here, I spoke with our Mayor Huggins and I also spoke with the individuals who make up the flight team of the so-called 'Redneck NASA.' We spent a long time debating what the next step would be, and we want our friends in the press to hear our decision first."

He was lying, but it didn't matter. He was lying, but he didn't care. This was worth it. He had them hanging on his every word now. Their attention was a white-hot blaze, and now he told the final lie that would become truth the moment he spoke it.

"We're going to build another rocket."

He paused to let it sink in. He'd never seen so many mouths hanging open before in his life.

"We are going to build another rocket and we are going to send it into space. And we are going to bring our people home. Jimmy, I want you to get on the ham and send a message up to those fellows."

And so that night, as the ISS passed over Melville, SC, the whole world heard the roar of the Rocket Zombies as a man with an upcountry accent more suited to fixing tractors than building rockets came over the airwaves loud and clear. And this is what he said:

"This is Redneck NASA broadcasting on all frequencies. This is Redneck NASA broadcasting on all frequencies. Hold on, *Space Jesus*. We're coming to bring you home."

ABOUT THE AUTHOR

Grady Hendrix is an award-winning novelist and screenwriter living in New York City. His books include *Horrorstör*, about a haunted IKEA, *My Best Friend's Exorcism, We Sold Our Souls*, and the *New York Times* bestsellers, *The Southern Book Club's Guide to Slaying Vampires* and *The Final Girl Support Group*. He's also the author of the non-fiction book, *Paperbacks from Hell*, a history of the horror paperback boom of the '70s and '80s, and his screenplays include *Mohawk* (2017) and *Satanic Panic* (2019).